BLUE AGAVE IMAGININGS

Josie,

I am so honored
to have met you and
to collaborate on your
East End Postcard Project!

Thank you,

BLUE AGAVE IMAGININGS

A COLLECTION OF SHORT STORIES BY

MANUEL NAVA LEAL

This collection of stories is a work of fiction. The names, characters and incidents portrayed within are entirely the product of the author's imagination. Any resemblance to actual persons, living or dead, is purely coincidental.

Balamku Press

BLUE AGAVE IMAGININGS
A Balamku Press book. ***January****/2020*

ISBN: 978-1-67815-120-1

Cover designed by: Mark Piñon

This book is dedicated to my best friend, Carlos Diaz Santana. RIP
See you soon, mi gran amigo!

ACKNOWLEDGEMENTS

The author wishes to thank and acknowledge the following persons:

Mark Piñon, for his beautifully enchanting cover design.

Carmen Avila, for her superb editing skills and supreme patience.

Art Ornelas, photographer extraordinaire.

Family and friends for your love, patience and guidance.

Mark Piñon – mark.pinon@gmail.com
Carmen Avila – avila.editor@gmail.com
Art Ornelas – art@tbhcenter.org

BLUE AGAVE IMAGININGS

Table of Contents

LEO

Near dusk, rain clouds rapidly grew denser, darker, full moon no longer visible. Fields of sorghum fenced in barbed wire on both sides of the black top road provided no shelter from the looming storm. Truck's battery had simply died, probably a dead cell or two. Hadn't seen a car or anyone else biking for a while, which was not unusual given that this was a long, isolated country road. I'd biked it a couple times in the past. I always searched out roads where there would be little if any traffic. I'd park my truck, take my bike out of the bed and ride for hours, enjoying the solitude, silence and sense of freedom experienced every time I biked. Unfortunately for me, I'd run out of time and luck this time. My cell phone's battery had also gone out earlier in the day. Hadn't worried about it then. I was now. My trusty bike would have to save my butt. Although my ass was sore, I had no choice but to continue a few more miles. Looking up at the fast approaching storm, hoping it wouldn't rain until I'd make it to shelter or getting a ride. Thunder rumbled, lightning was striking in the not too far distance. More afraid of lightning than anything I pedaled rapidly.

I rushed down the road which eventually meets with a busy highway, where with some luck, a good Samaritan might provide a lift. Nothing was in mind but the road ahead, a zone I go into when riding for long periods. I heard, then quickly felt the tire beneath me blow, it catapulted me toward the black tar, still hot from the summer's blazing sun. I did exactly the opposite of what I always cautioned bikers to avoid doing when experiencing a tumble, which is not to put your hands out to break your fall. "Hit the ground and roll," I'd religiously stated, but as is always the case; instinct overruled wisdom. My left wrist hurt slightly, hands and face were scraped. I was grateful for my helmet, which protected the rest of my head. The bike took the brunt of my weight, its front tire rim was bent. Assessing my bruises, cuts and sprain, carting my bike to the barbed wire fence, I lay it on its side next to a fence post, took my helmet off placed it under my arm and began the long trudge down the country road.

Sometime later, a dim yellow light led me to a small worn-down convenience store. Two old gas pumps sat sentinel below a canopy with a rusty "Texaco" filling station sign precariously hanging from a rusted bolt, it was spattered with bullet holes. A memory of passing it once vaguely arose in my mind, noticing the weathered boards barricading the front door also reminded. Rain caught me by surprise, I ran quickly and stood between the gas tanks. The fresh scent of wet earth engulfed my nostrils, penetrating my lungs. I loved that scent! It reminded me of my youth. Memories of playing in downpours, splashing in puddles, muddying my clothes. A happier time. I waited as the rain grew in intensity only to stop abruptly. Rain laden clouds still hovered above as I waited cautiously in case they let loose a thunder bolt or two. No more rain fell, and I began to resume my long trek. Taking a few steps, I suddenly heard noises coming from inside a beat-up trash dumpster whose lids were closed. Wondering if maybe a raccoon or two had found themselves trapped inside while scrounging for food. Being an animal lover, I decided to open both lids and help them out somehow. Not wanting to climb in and possibly get bit or scratched in the process, I looked about and saw an old weathered broom tucked behind a broken-down bench, grabbed it and walked over to the smelly dumpster and lifted one lid with the end of the broom stick lifting and pushing it back, then did the same with the other and stood back waiting. Nothing moved. I decided instead to place the broom inside and prop it against a wall to allow the raccoons to use it in their exit. The stench was bad, I stepped back a few feet to watch with anticipation. Again, no movement. Frustrated, thinking I'd done enough I began to turn away then saw fingers slowly come up and grip the edge of the dumpster. Realizing I may have interrupted a homeless person scrounging for food or something. I felt like jogging away, but curiosity kept my feet planted firmly to the ground. Another hand came up and grabbed the edge, I held my breath. It took a few moments before a dirty bald head peered out between both hands. Huge eyes looked towards me, although standing in darkness he might make me out. The man suddenly jumped up balancing his bare feet firmly on the edge of the dumpster. He squatted there, looking like a filthy old gargoyle. I couldn't believe what I was seeing! Why would a nearly naked man be scrounging inside a disgusting dumpster? He must be desperate or insane! Fear dissipated as I stood still. The thin bald man then stood on the edge and spread his arms wide. I nearly fainted! Beneath his arms, large folds of flesh spread out looking for all things like the membranes of a bat, like wings! Frozen to the spot, my mind raced trying to comprehend the sight. My heart pounded, head throbbed and my body trembled uncontrollably, I couldn't breathe. A scene from a horror movie ran through my mind. A vampire attacking and ripping a man to shreds after sucking the blood out of his throat. Not able to turn and run, I fell to my knees quietly weeping in fear, covering my mouth to stifle a cry as the creature jumped off and flew, no, no, glided towards me. My eyes shut tightly fearing the worst... nothing. I wiped my eyes and nose and looked up. He looked human, as he stood in front of me with a look of bemusement. His eyes were bloodshot, orange amber, skin dry old pale, splotched and heavily wrinkled.

I fell to the wet ground, bemused. He suddenly let out high-pitched laughter. Stunned, I felt embarrassed, childish. With both arms against his sides he looked normal. He wore a pair of dirty faded brown shorts and nothing else. I slowly rose to my feet wiping away tears and giggled like a small boy. He laughed louder. I wanted to turn and run, yet remained planted to the ground. My mind would not allow my body to move, needing to understand what I was seeing. I was afraid to speak and look at him directly. He stopped laughing and simply stared at me. We looked at one another for a long moment until a squeaky childlike voice escaped my throat.

"Hello. My, my name is Caleb. Bike blew a tire, I was hiking to the highway."

Silence.

I tried again, "My name is..."

"Caleb," was his whispered reply.

"Yes, Caleb."

"Caleb." He repeated.

"Yes." Was all I could muster.

He stared at me for a long time. I said nothing else, waiting for something, not knowing what to expect.

"Leo." He whispered.

"Leo." I repeated.

"Hello, Caleb."

"Hello Leo. I, I believe I was hallucinating or something, I may have imagined it, but I honestly thought you had...wings!"

"You did?"

"Yes, I feel like an idiot now that I've said it aloud."

"I do." He replied.

Once again, stunned into silence I stared blankly into his huge bloodshot amber eyes. My body trembled slightly and goose bumps rose on my cool skin.

"I have wings. They're part of me."

Swallowing, I asked curiously, "Why? How?"

"I was born like this." He answered in a childlike whisper.

Now I was embarrassed for asking and gently rocked back and forth on my heels.

"I was born like this," he repeated. They didn't know what to do when they saw me. They were scared. The doctor ran off. He didn't know what to say to my momma. The nurse who helped told my Daddy to sell me to a circus before she left. My Daddy thought about drowning me in the tub, but didn't cause I smiled."

"That's good, Leo" Is all I could say.

"He named me, Leo like my great-granddaddy. Said I'd be strong as a lion, like him! I'd be a great man, when I grew up!"

"Leo, good to meet you." I put my hand out, no longer fearful but still a bit shaken.

"Me too." He placed his cool, dry hand in mine.

"Do you live close by, Leo?

"Here! I live in the back. This was my Daddy's filling station, after he died my Uncle Jim took it and added to it, to help make it more of a store."

"It looks abandoned."

"Been closed a long while. When my uncle died there was no one else but me. He never showed me how to run it. I didn't know what to do, how to run it. People were scared of me."

"What about your mother, why didn't she run it or at least help you?

"Mama left us some time after I was born. She wouldn't look after me, afraid to touch me.

Daddy didn't have to tell me why she left. Once I could talk and read and write, he showed me some pictures and letters she sent for a while before they stopped Never did know what happened to her. Maybe got a new family, maybe up and died!"

"Sorry, Leo. Must have been tough for you as a child."

"Still is." He answered sadly.

"I'm sorry, that was so stupid of me. Of course, you still hurt. Sorry, Leo."

"That's alright Caleb, you didn't mean nothing by it."

"Got any water, Leo? Throat's dry."

"There's a hose over there, come on!"

"You're drinking from a hose?"

"Yeah, sink and tub don't work no more, got plugged up or something."

"Will you show me around?"

"You won't like it inside, it's bad, really bad No one else been in there a long time. I'm not good at cleaning, I don't clean nothing."

"That's ok Leo. I'm not very tidy myself."

We walked to the back of the building and I saw a lean-to against the back wall. Leo pulled at a screen door and it nearly fell off its hinges. He asked me to prop it open while he entered, returning with a candle in each hand. Leo handed me one and asked me to follow him inside. He'd lit several candles making the shelter more frightening as shadows jumped about in the darkness. The stench was putrid! I covered my nose and mouth with my bare arm.

The place was filthy, stacked with old boxes, yellowed girlie magazines, newspapers, fast food paper sacks and cups. Rats skittered off as soon as candlelight caught their eyes. Needed to stoop, as the ceiling was bowed by weight and gravity. Leo came back and asked if I was hungry. I shook my head no. I suppose he'd grown immune to the stench. It smelled of spoiled meat, fish and death. Leo lurked about with candle held firmly in hand. I could see nerves, veins and splotches on his "wings," as he lifted his arm to light the way. Afraid to touch anything I asked Leo if he'd mind, my going back outside. Turning away, a hand strongly gripped my right shoulder and my sphincter instinctively tightened. I wanted to run but slowly turned to face him instead. He pointed to a dark corner with a bony finger, holding the candle out with his other hand. I shimmied towards the dark corner not knowing what to expect. He released my arm and quickly moved around me holding the candle above an old dust covered bed. There, dressed in filthy, oil splotched coveralls lay a long and shriveled gray-haired mummy of a man.

"Uncle Jim." Leo whispered.

Shivers trembled through me in the stifling heat, horrified at the sight.

"Uncle Jim? I slowly asked. "How long? How long has he been like that?

"Long time." Leo replied in a whisper.

"Leo, I need to go and bring some help. I'll hurry back! Ok, Leo? What would you like me to bring you? Clothes? Shoes? Food? What have you been eating?"

"Most times, people come by and toss their food into my dumpster. I got'a hurry and get it before the coons and rats do! They can smell it a long way off. I got'a wait till dark most times. I got'a pile of rocks and I throw'em at'm when they get close. I'm good at hittin'em, but I only want'a keep them away. Sometimes people throw away food they didn't even touch! I get drinks and all!"

"Leo, Leo! I'm going for help, ok? I'll hurry and get back soon! You need help, Leo."

"I'm good, Caleb. I'm do'n good!"

"Yes, you've done good, but you need fresh food, clothes and you need to see a doctor too!"

"No doctors! Noooo doctors!" Fuck'em all!

I needed air, needed out of that stifling room. My lungs burned from the stench, my heart beat wildly! Leo must be insane, I thought! He'd probably been insane for, who knows how long? Poor Leo, I'd grown sad and fearful of him.

"I need to go outside, Leo! I'm feeling sick to my stomach and I don't want to vomit in here!"

"Go, Caleb! Go! Go on! Leave like everyone else! GO!"

Not wanting to run I took slow deliberate long steps. My legs were now shaking uncontrollably and I didn't want him to suddenly attack. Leo now frightened me more than before. My eyes teared up again as I bent forward, gripping my stomach.

"Please, I need to go outside!" I pleaded while slowly taking longer strides to the entrance. My heart pounded against my chest nearing the screen door. Leo squeezed his bony fingers into my shoulder and again... nearly fainted!

"I'm sorry, Caleb." Leo spoke sympathetically. "Go on outside! Hurry!" He gently pushed me.

After lifting the screen door, I ran out and fell to my knees onto the moist earth. I dry wretched and gasped for fresh air before placing my forehead to the ground. A cool hand patted my back gently, soothing me as I rocked on my elbows and knees.

"I'm sorry I took you in there, Caleb. It smells bad, I know. It smelled bad when Uncle Jim died. Just didn't know what to do."

"It's alright Leo, I understand."

"I'm glad you came here, Caleb. I'm glad you came. I never thought I'd make a friend. I never had any friends, you know?"

"I'm a friend, Leo. OK? You and I are friends!"

"You're my friend, Caleb!"

Leo knelt and his body shook as he sobbed. I reached over and hugged his bare shoulders. I felt such empathy for Leo's poor soul. I grabbed his arm feeling the loose flesh that was his "wing" and helped raise him to his feet. His toenails were long, dry, cracked and bent like an animal's claws, his fingernails looked no better. Leo needed help. My friends would help me, too. Hell! I'd take him to a doctor myself once, I'd convince him it was ok!

"Can I come with you?" Leo asked quietly.

I froze, not knowing how to respond to his question.

"I promise I won't open my arms." He stated forlornly.

"No, Leo, I'm sorry. Not right now. I must get home first. Remember, I'm walking. I promise to return first thing in the morning. Ok?

"Ok." Leo replied sadly. He bent down picked up my helmet and handed it to me.

"Leo, I promise to come back, ok?" I strapped my helmet on and patted his shoulders.

"Ok, Caleb. My friend." Leo smiled, took my hand into his and shook it firmly.

Walked off feeling as exhilarated, as when riding my bike without a care in the world, breeze in my face and a smile on my lips. I couldn't wait to get back to Austin and bring Leo much needed help. His mind needed fixing and body needed proper nourishment. More than anything, he needed a friend. Glancing over my shoulder once more, I waved back. Leo stood on the store's rooftop and waved grandly in the bright orange moonlight. He then spread his arms wide. Leo must be smiling, I felt his joy! Waving broadly, I jumped into the air a couple of times. Leo jumped off the roof and slipped into the air. Seeing him gliding high above the rooftop, I hardly believed my eyes! He went higher, and higher! He flew in front of the huge harvest moon, then brought his arms smartly down to his sides. He fell through the air as I watched with anticipation, knowing he'd open his arms wide and swoop back up once more, propelling himself way above the rooftop back to the full moon and possibly higher! I heard him yell, "Goodbye, Caleb! Goodbye!" Then he thunderously crashed through the rooftop below. I heard the resounding crash, then a sudden "Whoosh" lit the store in massive orange yellow flames!

"LEO! LEEEOOO!" *Shouting franticly, I sprinted back.* ***"LEEEEEOOOOO! LEEEEEOOOOO!"***

When I reached the store, it was crumbled and smoldering with patches of flames here and there. The fire had quickly consumed the old wooden building. It must have been the open candles. I sobbed aloud thinking of my friend, Leo. He must have been in so much pain. I'd been too quick to get away, not fully understanding his heartache. I was sitting on the moist warm ground silently crying when sirens neared. I rose to my feet wiping away the tears and snot, as a fire truck and an ambulance approached.

END

GENIUS

As things came into focus and blurry visions came into shape, I screamed. The terror that engulfed me was so intense that I passed out although my eyes were wide open.

My mind could not understand what was happening.

How did we end up here? What had we been doing, before this?

I came to, again and again the visions grew clearer; my wife was being dissected right in front of me.

Get away from her!!!! Get away from her!!!! Leave her alone!!!! Don't touch her you bastard!!! Leave her alone!!!!

I can't hear myself...

Why can't I hear myself?

Oh, God... Please don't. Please don't do that. Please, please let her go...

My mind comes in and out of darkness. Although my eyes are wide open, darkness keeps coming back again and again. The lights in this room are bright, so bright and yet I see darkness repeatedly. Every time I come to, I see this, doctor? Maniac? Psycho? Cut her, play with her. I want to cry and maybe I am, but I can't feel it happening.

How long has this been happening?

I can't move.

Am I tied down, like Ann is?

The terror is so intense. The sense of utter helplessness is excruciating. The inability to rescue my wife hurts even more deeply. I could never have imagined such terror and anguish.

Why can't I move? Why won't my eyes shut?

My eyes won't close. I don't want to see her this way.

I don't understand. What have we done to deserve this? Why? Why, us? Why? WHY????

My arms won't move my body feels dead.

What have you done to us?

That asshole is playing with Ann's breasts, slapping them, pinching them, biting them.

Oh God, where are you? Why is he doing this? How can you let this happen?

I realize my hopelessness. There is nothing I can do. This psycho is doing what he wants and there is nothing I or anyone can do to stop him.

God? There is no God.

How long has this been going on?

Oh no. No, no nooooo. Don't do that. Don't do that! Please leave her alone!

Ann, Ann. Oh no. She feels. She feels everything. Oh no!

I can see suffering in her eyes. They're clamped open like my own. She can't move but she's feeling the pain.

Ann…my love…please die. Go, just go. I'm with you, I'm with you. Please baby…please go on.

Who are you, you bastard? Why are you doing this to us!

Please kill her! Don't torture her anymore! Kill her! Kill her you son-of-a-bitch!

Ahhhhhhhhh, why? Why? Why? Oh nooooooooo! Let her be!

He, he's finally done with my Ann… He cut her heart out of her and the motherfucker bit into it! He smiled! That bastard smiled as he bit into her heart…

There is no God! If I get a chance to see a God, I'll beat the shit out of it! You, no good bastards! You sick fucking bastards! You're just as sick as this son-of-a-bitch!

What is going on? That bastard left the room and my Ann is still on that table. My love, my poor, poor lovely wife… I don't care what you do to me now you, sick fuck! I don't care, I want to die and be with my baby, Ann…

Where are you? Where are you, you, sick fucker! Oh, God! There he is! What are you doing with her body now, you fuck? Come back! Come back!

He's back.

What did you do with my Ann? Where is she? Where?

Oh, God. He's coming this way. He's coming to me!

I was wrong, Ann couldn't have felt that scalpel. I don't feel a thing. He's cutting into me and I don't feel a fucking thing! Why, don't I feel anything? I'm so glad to know she didn't feel anything. Who the fuck, are you? I've never seen you before. Why did you pick us? What did we do? Why, us? Oh, God he's cut my hands off! He's shaking my hand in greeting. He's laughing and talking to himself. This fucker is really, sick!

He's injecting me with something. He knows, I'm starting to feel something. I can feel the cold of my feet. It's working, I don't feel anything again. Why does he do this if he knows we don't feel pain? He knows we're mentally aware and he feeds on the fear he sees in our eyes. Maybe that's all he wants? Maybe, he's afraid of the screams? What pleasure does this fuck, get? What does he feel?

He's cutting out my eye! There it is! He's playing with it! He's laughing and talking to it.

What's that behind him? Someone slowly coming up behind him. It's a man, and he's holding a gun! Yes! Yes! Kill this motherfucker! Shoot him! Shoot this motherfucker!

I woke up in a hospital a few days later. My eye was reattached, is what I heard them say, although I can't see since it's patched up. I feel as though I can talk but I don't want to. I know it won't be long before the police come to talk with me. I don't know what I'll tell them. How could this have happened? Why us? I just don't know...

The detectives are thoughtful, professional. I appreciate their taking it slow with me. I'm still worn out. What's left of my body is worn down.

I don't know what happened or how. My wife and I went to bed as usual and then we awoke in that freak bastard's lab. Where is that sick fuck? Where is he!

Yes, sir. I'm calm, now. No, he tortured my wife, and played with her body before he cut her heart out. No, I couldn't feel a thing, I was drugged. No, I've never heard of that drug before. I couldn't feel anything. It was my mind! What I felt was fear and loathing! My experience just as my wife's, was mental. Excruciating anguish, anger and fear.

Why won't you tell me anything about that monster? Who is he? Where is he, now? Is he alive? A, doctor? He's, a doctor? How is that possible? He killed himself? How? How?

The detectives told me that the bastard was a doctor. He poisoned himself. What a coward. He'd been doing this for years. He was finally caught, but I don't know how. I don't really, care. I'm grateful he's dead. I hope he's being tortured in hell...

My hands have been reattached, the detectives placed them in a freezer to preserve them. Thank, God!

God... God... Do I even believe in a God, anymore? After this? Where was God when that fucker was killing others? Where was God when Ann was, suffering and dying? Where was God when I was getting cut to pieces? Why didn't God stop that motherfucker from killing? Why do we have to believe in a God? I don't want to think of God anymore... There is no God as far as I am concerned!

Yes, Ann was pregnant. Yes, I saw what that monster did to my Ann. He didn't touch her stomach, I'm glad of that. Yes, the baby was due, in weeks. What!

When I held my daughter in my arms, I could not believe it. How could that be? How did she survive in Ann after all she went through? The drugs were enough to kill our baby girl. She suffered withdrawals. Poor baby, had to go through withdrawals and special care for months. They never told me, never... They wanted me to recover sufficiently, before they would break the news. My baby, girl...

It's been three years and my hands are slowly gaining strength. I can do more than I imagined possible. Those surgeons are miracle workers. I can't say enough about them. That bastard monster, I was told, was a surgeon himself. I wonder what could have possessed him to go insane. Supposedly he was a genius. The best surgeon in the state, yet no one truly knew who and what he was.

Annie, our daughter, is three! I can't believe how beautiful she is! She looks just like her mommy... I must raise her to be a good girl. I must watch her closely and keep her from harm, as much as possible. She's our treasure! *God, what a beautiful child!*

God... God... Yes, I believe in God. He preserved our baby... God saved us both... I must believe, despite what we went through! Ann, Annie, I will always cherish your memory, I will love you forever. I will see you again! Please, Ann help me believe in God, once more!

END

NAPOLEON'S FINE ANTIQUE STORAGE

Napoleon Beene had loved antiques since childhood. Both his grandmother and mother had owned and operated antique shops for decades in an exclusive section of Houston, Texas. His early fancy had been piqued by early Americana furniture, with a penchant for Hepplewhite, better known as the Federal style of early American furniture. Each piece discovered was akin to a gift to the effeminate and delicate man. Napoleon was an effeminate man, slight of stature with exquisitely manicured hands, sporting a richly black-dyed pencil-thin mustache, thinning hair (also dyed) and drawn back, properly pasted down with rose scented grease; added to his haughty demeanor was a slight British tilt in a high-pitched voice. His hand-tailored suits, ties, kerchiefs, socks and shoes were Italian, shirts British, undergarments, French silk. He fancied himself a man of culture and style, such as that now missing, from what he considered, an advertisement t-shirt and tennis shoe wearing sub-culture. He frowned on just about all things new. Napoleon happened to be, a successful murderer.

Mr. Beene's mother, Hortencia Beene, had entrusted her life savings to an embezzler who had regaled her with promises of immense returns on investments in diamond mines in South America. He'd convinced her of vast freshly discovered diamond mines which rivaled the prolific mines in the African continent. He'd lavished her with both excellently cut real and fake examples which she never failed to wear on their dinner outings. She had encouraged several dear friends and clients to invest. The scheme unraveled in time, leaving her and all investors in dire straits! The embezzler eventually "jumped" from the roof of a luxury hotel, a supposed suicide, some suspected an angry, vengeful investor had taken justice into his own hands. Regardless of the circumstances, Napoleon found himself in a supremely life altering position. His anger towards his mother and her foolishness was quite intense. He stole the little money she had hidden in her "safe place," pawned the few valuable pieces of jewelry left in her personal collection, and finally burned down the family antique shop, failing to rescue his frail mother from the resulting inferno. The conflagration, was of course, "accidental," according to Napoleon who, had been at an outing with friends. The insurance company naturally balked, eventually paying off a hefty sum. Napoleon purchased a small building which he converted into his own antique shop with his windfall. He, of course, sought to sell to his mother's former clients. Unfortunately, he was not as successful as he had anticipated.

Napoleon did manage to snag a few customers some of which had been his mother's oldest former clients. Matrons of wealth wishing to bequeath their children and grandchildren with their antique holdings, children who shared little if any interest in "ancient, dreary, useless furniture." Napoleon found himself purchasing much of the heirlooms for pennies and at times at no cost. He also resorted to murder.

His first victim was a Mrs. Oates, a homebound invalid whom he befriended and visited occasionally, bringing unique little dishes personally prepared for her. He'd ingratiated himself in other ways as well, serving to read personal mail out loud, tend to her flower garden and clean up, bathe and feed her old feeble lap dog, Fifi. He despised dogs especially Fifi and eventually fed her finely crushed glass in a divine pâté of turkey meat. Mrs. Oates cried her heart out as she had hoped to outlive her beloved pet and gift the kind Mr. Beene her loving Fifi. Mr. Beene's sadness at Fifi's demise was a stellar acting performance, surprising himself. He'd dug a special grave in a lush area under a dense tree canopied spot next to one of Mrs. Oates favorite gardens. He read a passage from an old worn King James Bible which pleased Mrs. Oates to no end. The charade continued for some months causing Napoleon intense consternation. The old bitch refused to die! He hated lifting her huge fat body to and from bed and into that damned wheelchair, a relic as old as she! Not wishing to arouse suspicion, he refused to resort to poisons, gas stove leaks or the old pillow suffocation method. Napoleon had instead chosen to inject a bit of water laden with a bubble of air using an old syringe which he'd found while rummaging through boxes of items in his shop. He had hoped the bubble would kill her instantly. Instead, he found her face down on the kitchen floor, arms trapped beneath her fat grotesque body. She'd been unable to lift herself even slightly. She'd apparently attempted to reach for something on the counter and had fallen as a result. He knew her panic button lay under her fat heavy body which, she'd been unable to reach. Thank goodness for his luck, he thought! As she lay there softly pleading for help, he rifled through her personal belongings, finding cash, a collection of rare coins, and a handful of gems and jewelry in a tin container on the topmost shelf of her bedroom closet. He also discovered a loaded Colt .45 under her mattress and an original Bowie knife which he would later sell for a few thousand dollars. Hours passed as she moaned and weakly struggled to lift herself. She wept as she softly called out for help while Napoleon prepared a pot of tea, enjoyed a few crumpets with sweet cream and waited patiently for her demise. Slowly growing impatient Napoleon thought about placing a plastic bag over her head and be done with it; however, he reconsidered. Thinking it best to let her die normally. As nightfall approached he rose, cleaned up after himself and left Mrs. Oates tearfully pleading for help.

Returning two days later he instantly knew she'd finally died upon entering the house. The smell of defecate and urine was intensely horrid! He covered his nose and mouth with his silk kerchief and placed the toe of his right foot against her forehead gently pushing it back, hoping for no reaction. Mrs. Oates had thankfully perished. After more rummaging through the house, in case he had inadvertently missed anything, he hysterically called 911 to report his find, afterwards, he dialed her only daughter and using the same hysterical high-pitched voice (with a bit of teeth gnashing and crying added for good measure,) broke the sad news of her dear mother's accidental demise. After hanging up, Napoleon stepped out for fresh air and sat casually on a garden bench awaiting the police. He practiced a tearful act until their arrival.

Napoleon found himself in the antique storage business by sheer luck. One of his mother's beloved customers asked Napoleon if he had room to store some furniture pieces she had little room for, in one of her homes. He was about to decline but was suddenly hit with an idea and gladly offered his assistance for a tiny fee, "of course," which she agreed upon without the usual squabble. She allowed him the courtesy of inspecting the pieces in her mansion. Napoleon was shocked to see the largest collection of Hepplewhite he'd ever seen! He swooned at the sight. On wobbly legs he inspected every piece, lovingly touching and admiring each. Afterwards, he contacted a reliable business acquaintance to move the large exquisite collection. Rushing to his shop, he began clearing space in an extra storage area. If necessary, he'd rent storage nearby. He tenderly cried as the Hepplewhite was gently unloaded.

Each time he entered the storage area Napoleon ran his hands over the finely crafted mahogany furniture. He loved their straight form and rigid lines. He dreamed of possessing it all! His desire was immense! An idea began percolating in his devilish mind. He smiled at the thought as his thin nostrils sniffed the air, inhaling the scent of aged wood and linseed oil, detesting its use and smell. "Idiots." he whispered to himself, "always applying too much on these delicate pieces!" His scheme was a simple one. "The best crimes are the simplest," reassuring himself.

Mrs. Daniel Goss Ford III, claimed to be a descendant of one of the first wealthy settlers of Tejas, the original name for the present state of Texas. Her family had been invited to visit Tejas and Mexico City after meeting an influential Mexican Ambassador who'd been ordered to Tennessee on a fact-finding mission for his President, Anastasio Bustamante y Oseguera. Once emigrating to central Tejas, they chose to stay. It would be a few years before the state of Texas was formed after which they purchased thousands of acres of land, which was the start of their dynasty. The old matriarch had become widowed early in her marriage. Mr. Daniel Ford III had suffered a massive heart attack in one of Dallas' fanciest hotels; found with a suffocated young black prostitute under the massively rotund man. The discovery was squelched by the influential family and the indecent Mr. Ford III was provided a large decent funeral. "Bess," as she preferred being addressed, had stoically suffered the personal shame throughout her years. Napoleon could care less about her family history. His heart was in owning Bess' Hepplewhite collection. He began insinuating himself into her life bit by bit. Unlike Mrs. Oates, Bess was a lithe and handsome woman. She walked with the aid of a cane on occasion and would occasionally accept Napoleon's arm as support. Bess shyly asked for the name of his cologne, which she was mad about! He, being quite vain whispered the expensive name into her ear, pressing his pointy nose against her soft wrinkled neck. He felt like retching but held firm. She on the other hand smelled of old sweaty age Lavender perfume. Bess was kind and thoughtful, she craved attention and lavished Napoleon with little valueless trinkets which he feigned a love for. Nevertheless, he endured her companionship and often found himself enjoying the attention she poured on him. Once while window shopping at the Galleria, he pointed out a watch he happened to like and she surprised him with it at breakfast the next morning. Napoleon was shocked at the surprise gift. He intended on kissing her cheek when she suddenly turned to face him and kissed his lips. Shocked once more, Napoleon tenderly returned the kiss. Later he excused himself, rushing to a lavatory where he wiped his lips clean with a soft soap. He frowned at his reflection growing furious at himself for having to endure such acts.

It wasn't long after their first kiss that Bess began hinting of a desire for intimacy. Napoleon didn't know if he had it in him to act upon her desires. He did his best to avoid the subject but she persisted without being too forward. While sitting together she would on occasion place her hand near his crotch and gently run her fingers between his legs. Bess knew how to arouse sensations and once, Napoleon's body reacted involuntarily, an erection arose as Bess touched his groin and she quickly squeezed. Napoleon knew he had to perform as never-before and unzipped. Bess smiled and took him into her mouth. Even after Napoleon had come, which had taken some time; Bess would not let go of his penis. She hadn't been with a man in decades and was not about to let this moment end that quickly. She asked Napoleon to unzip her dress and his hands shook while doing so. Napoleon kept his eyes closed as she stood and let the dress fall to the floor. Bess placed her hands on his chin and asked him to open his eyes.

Napoleon nearly cried as he forced his eyes open, shocked to see what was before him. Bess had been hiding a nicely proportioned and well-preserved body. He stared at her breasts then reached to tenderly pinch her nipples before wrapping his lips upon one. Bess closed her eyes enjoying his mouth and hands as one made its way down and between her legs. It was difficult for Napoleon to fathom the experience. He grew erect once more and penetrated Bess. She screamed and scratched his neck while he pushed himself into her. She was unbelievably tight. Napoleon couldn't understand how this was possible, Bess was in her late seventies! After they were completely spent, Bess whispered that she had not been with a man since her husband's death, nearly forty-five years past. Napoleon asked her why she had done so now, and she replied, "It was your cologne, my dear." For a moment, Napoleon felt uneasy. He had expected to hear something like, "Your mustache, your physique, or your smile," anything but "cologne." He reminded himself of the Hepplewhite and his agenda and readjusted his thoughts. He suddenly felt childish and turned to face Bess. She had been studying him closely and suddenly felt foolish. She grabbed her dress and covered herself to her neck. Napoleon took her hands into his and kissed them. Bess fell in love at that moment.

Months dragged on and Napoleon felt more and more constricted. He harbored several scenarios in mind becoming more and more desperate as time passed. He had nearly pushed her off a third-floor balcony one evening as they entertained company. Her lady friends eyed him with suspicion and the man scorned him. He felt uncomfortable most times but acted happily when Bess was within eyeshot. She had a habit of tightly holding his arm as she dragged him nearer to friends. He'd been practicing a deeper timber to his voice but believed her friends could see through the ruse. He started walking with a swagger attempting to impress the men, it didn't help. He found himself edging closer and closer to the cocktail bar. The bartenders didn't mind the trivial conversations as they continued to pour him drinks. Napoleon began drinking more and more and at one point nearly toppled a planter, embarrassing Bess to no end. That evening in their bed, Bess let him know of her embarrassment. He nearly laughed out loud but had enough sense not to do so. He grew more and more wary of the arrangement and vowed that evening, to kill her.

Napoleon was inspecting a furniture delivery and watched as the men carried the pieces one by one on wooden pallets, moving them easily with a pallet jack. A thought came to mind, an idea to finally rid himself of Bess. He'd have to invite her to the shop and that could prove difficult. He purchased a small pallet jack and loaded a heavy armoire on a wooden skid making sure it tilted precariously. He raised the jack just high enough that if it fell, the entire piece would fall flat.

Bess grew worried when Napoleon called to tell her with great concern, that several pieces of her collection had suffered slight damage when a sprinkler line had sprung a minor leak.

Bess entered the storage area in a huff, she was not in the best of moods and nudged Napoleon onward. He turned to face her with a look of mock rage and asked her to slow down and not push. Bess hesitated briefly then suddenly slapped him! With a burst of rage, Napoleon returned the slap which caused Bess to cry out in pain. He quickly pulled her to him and held her firmly against his chest.

"Bess," he began, "I am so sorry. As you know, the damage was quite accidental. I understand your anger, the damage pains me as well. You know I too, cherish your collection!" Bess stopped crying and held Napoleon tightly against herself.

"I apologize Napoleon. I am so fond of my pieces, it took me years to find and select each one."

"Yes, you've mentioned that several times."

"I have? I'm such a silly girl! Of course, I have. I do apologize for my behavior. Will you forgive me, my love?"

"Nothing to forgive, my dear. Please, follow me, to the back."

Napoleon took her hand and led her towards the armoire. He stopped just past the tilting bulk and asked Bess to close her eyes for a moment. She giggled like a small child and complied with her lover's command. Bess held her arms to her chest anxiously awaiting her surprise as the armoire came barreling down on her thin frame.

Napoleon composed himself before running outside to frantically call out at Bess's chauffeur "Howard," to call 911 immediately!

Howard called right away then ran after Napoleon, to assist with Bess. They both struggled to move the piece but Napoleon kept screaming that they were causing Bess more pain. Howard would not stop lifting the heavy piece, he asked Napoleon to find something to help prop it up at the very least! Napoleon ran off and casually looked about for a pole or pipe to use, while taking his time. He finally returned with a useless broomstick that angered Howard. He screamed at Napoleon and then ran off to look for something more appropriate. He returned with a metal pipe which he pushed under the armoire and then lifted. Napoleon grabbed Bess by the arm and dragged her lifeless body out from underneath. Howard let the armoire fall and fell back on his haunches shaking and satisfied. He was angry with Napoleon, he suspected him of causing Bess's death but said nothing. Later he would tell the police of his suspicions.

Napoleon shut himself away for a few weeks, only attending Bess's funeral. That day he cried and mourned loudly, to the point that he dramatically hugged Bess's coffin, embarrassing her daughter immensely. The press covered the fancy service and a photographer snapped Napoleon's dramatic moment, further angering the daughter.

While Napoleon hid from the public, he began to surreptitiously move some of the best Hepplewhite pieces into a rental storage facility not far from his shop. He smiled and unconsciously clapped his hands like a child as he viewed his stolen treasures. It would be a long wait before he would take them out and move them into his home.

Months later, Napoleon was summoned to a deposition, where he would be asked questions concerning the odd circumstance of Mrs. Daniel Goss Ford III's untimely death. Napoleon feared the coming proceeding and began drinking again to calm his nerves. His hands shook while thinking up things to say. He practiced phrases over and over so as, not to change them in any way. He understood that he would be asked the same questions over and over, attempting to trip him and catch him in a fabrication. He spoke the phrases out loud, he repeated them like chants. He drank and then drank more. He would fall asleep, imagining the scenario, until he'd awaken in cold sweats.

The offices were luxurious, the table and chairs were of modern style, he immediately recognized the Davis Allen signature design. Allen had been the designer selected for the Lyndon Baines Johnson Library in Austin. Napoleon was impressed although, he was not much into the modern designs. He leaned back into his seat and waited impatiently for the inquisition to begin. He was tapping his fingers furiously when the lawyers entered and introduced themselves.

As Napoleon walked away from the offices, he felt a huge sense of relief sweep through his body. He took a deep breath and smiled smugly to himself. He felt sure of his performance and was assured by the attorneys that his cooperation was greatly appreciated. He headed home to celebrate his victory.

The next morning, he arrived at his shop to find two large moving vans awaiting his arrival. As he approached the front door, Bess's daughter, Tammy suddenly appeared accompanied by one of the attorney's he'd seen but not spoken to at the deposition and two county deputies, who produced a warrant for the Hepplewhite. Napoleon was caught by surprise and angrily confronted Tammy and the attorney. She ignored his behavior and requested a deputy to ask Napoleon for the key. Napoleon slapped his keyring into the deputy's hand who pushed past him to unlock the door. Tammy produced a list of furnishings to Napoleon's surprise. He hadn't been given a list by Bess and suddenly was petrified with fear.

As Tammy and her attorney walked the premises, it became clear to her that some pieces were missing. She would on occasion glare angrily at Napoleon.

The deputies kept a close watch over Napoleon which made him feel claustrophobic. He wanted to step away but as he moved about, a deputy would follow closely. As Tammy and her attorney finished inventorying the furniture, they showed the deputy's the list of items that were present and obviously those which were missing. One deputy approached Napoleon and in a whisper asked about the missing furniture. Napoleon feigned ignorance and they all stared without saying a word.

Napoleon tearfully watched as the moving men entered his storage area and began the slow tedious process of removing the remaining Hepplewhite. His body shook as he saw piece after piece leave the building. He wanted to strangle Tammy and her attorney right there in front of the deputies. He envisioned tearing out her eyes and stomping her head into the ground. Tammy stared just as angrily, probably wishing to do the same to him. She smugly smiled at Napoleon when she saw the tears run down his face. She knew that he'd murdered her mother and she'd make damn sure he'd die on a Huntsville table with a lethal dose running through his cold veins!

As the last van drove away with the patrol car following, Napoleon fell to the floor and cried like a baby. How did he not think of Bess having created a fucking list? Why hadn't he thought of it? How stupid of me! I should have known! He repeated over and over to himself. He knew Tammy would next have him served to produce the missing pieces. He couldn't kill Tammy, could he? Why not? He had to kill her! There wasn't much choice. He didn't know where she lived but he did know her favorite eating and shopping places. Bess had always gossiped about Tammy's habits. He had to come up with something.

Napoleon sat at a corner table of an outdoor Café, sipping a dark Italian espresso from a tiny porcelain cup. He saw Tammy enter a small boutique across the street. She was shopping at the usual spots and sported several fancy bags from trendy shops. Napoleon left the Café and made his way to a parking lot around the corner from it. He had "borrowed," a car from an elderly client who was unaware of the theft. He drove around in circles hoping to catch Tammy at the right spot. He'd rounded the block thrice when he saw her at the very corner across from the Café. Tammy was rummaging through her Dior purse for her sunglasses which were presently resting on top of her head. As she stepped into the crosswalk, she hesitated and reached to touch her glasses, she let out a laugh and dropped them to her nose as the pilfered car hit her broadside, sending her into the air only to land face-first onto the pavement a few feet from the crosswalk. Tammy bloodied and broken, struggled to prop herself onto an elbow, the automobile then hit her head and ran over her body, driving away at great speed. No one could say definitively what the driver looked like as most pedestrians and Café customers were holding conversations with someone or were busy looking at their cell phones or tablets.

Hours after Tammy's murder, Napoleon relaxed and drank a dark red Chianti in one of Mrs. Oates' flower gardens. He stared down at the spot at which he'd buried little old, Fifi. He smiled at the thought of her suffering, remembering the bloody mess he'd cleaned up minutes before she died. A sense of freedom currently settled in his mind. He felt free of Bess and all other constraints. He'd wait patiently for the coming auction of Bess's collection, now that there were no heirs to her fortune. He felt giddy thinking of the Hepplewhites return. Napoleon didn't know of, or expect anyone to bid for the furniture. He felt confident of that.

The next morning as he inserted the door key to the shop, Napoleon felt a strong handhold and squeeze his arm tightly. He was shoved and pushed firmly against the door, his arms were then pulled roughly and twisted against his back. He felt, then heard handcuffs lock tightly around his wrists, which caused him to let out a little yelp and wince in pain.

At the police station he was shown photos of himself entering and driving off in the stolen car away from his client's residence. Another series of photos showed him parking the car in the lot and driving it out minutes later. Finally, a series showing the car hit and run over Tammy. Napoleon had not counted on a private investigator's tracking of his moves. The investigator had been hired by his last victim. He hadn't expected Napoleon to kill Tammy and tried his best to assist her at the scene. Tammy had died in his arms knowing Napoleon was responsible for her and her mother's deaths and would finally be held to account.

Napoleon Beene's appearance was startling to all who had known him and who are now present in his final moments. He wore black framed glasses was pale, gaunt, bald and clean shaven as he lay on a gurney clearly fearful as tears flowed down the edges of his face. He rejected a chaplain, refusing to speak to his guards or the warden, whom he disdained. He'd refused a last meal choosing instead a room temperature Perrier. Strapped to a gurney, attached to an EKG monitor he smiles and winces as IV's are inserted into his hands. Time passes slowly as the EKG monitor beeps repeatedly. The IVs deliver the barbiturate, paralytic, and potassium solution into his bloodstream. Napoleon dies without a smile. Tammy would have been pleased.

END

IMPLEMENT

Chapter One

At the time, the road ahead of me was just as empty of vehicles as it had been for miles previous, so I was quite surprised to see a large object coming into view through my bug splattered windshield. The object was disc shaped and to my stunned surprise appeared to be hovering a few yards above the blacktop, or rather just above the road but closer to the shoulder. A dull fear ran through my mind that eventually moved slowly down my spine and chillingly filled my entire being. I tried to look away and found that I could not, for some inexplicable reason I felt as though whatever was in that object, was keeping me focused on it. Don't ask why, but I seemed to feel, no, that's not the right word, I somehow *knew* that I had been given this opportunity. Why I was even on the road at the time was a mystery, as I had awoken that morning with a yearning to drive that is unexplainable. Nevertheless, I sat there with a sense of wonder and awe with a good bit of fear of the unknown object that somehow emitted a glow without obvious lighting. It was not too far ahead of my car maybe about half a mile away and I'd say that it was maybe about thirty to forty feet wide and five to six feet at its widest central point.

The sun was just peeking over the horizon and its rays lit up the ranchlands around me with the most beautiful golden and reddish fingers pointing to the darkness to my right. As I looked back to the object, it moved away so quickly that all I saw was its glow growing smaller and finally disappearing directly into the darkness at about a fifteen-degree angle. My first thought was that if a jetliner had been in its path, they surely would have collided. I sat in my car for a long while before remembering the horse or calf on the side of the road. I slowly opened my door and stepped out into the coolness of the morning, the air made my body shiver and instantly goose pimples rose on my exposed arms and neck. Reaching into the backseat I grabbed my windbreaker, pulling it on just as a cooler breeze blew against my face. The wind carried with it, the scent of horse. I knew then, without getting near that what I'd seen below that hovering object had been a horse's body.

The cool gravel crackled below the soles of my boots as I slowly approached the dead horse. Noticing that the air around me failed to carry the stench of death, I quickly turned and ran back to my car and grabbed my camera, having seen that the horse was missing the side of its face which was not against the ground. My hands shook as I took the first picture and continued shaking as I walked around the corpse, taking photos of it and the ground surrounding it. I began methodically searching for footprints or markings on the soft dirt shoulder and found odd looking three toed prints which I could not easily identify.

I'm quite familiar with the animals of my state of Texas and have never seen prints that resembled these, even in the nature books and historical manuals which I found surprising. I was bewildered at finding no blood on the scene, not one drop. The horse was coated with a light-colored mud that did not match the dark loam of the shoulder, it appeared to have struggled or had been sleeping on its right side before it was killed. I say killed because the animal had been mutilated.

On closer inspection, the horse was a young mare which, had once gone under the knife. An old surgical scar nearly sixteen inches long with clean stitches which had healed well, ran alongside her belly and then turned at a right angle further inside another five. Whoever the veterinarian had been they'd done a fine job, unfortunately, someone else had done a finer job of removing half of her facial skin including the eye, optical nerve, veins, blood vessels, and tongue, exposing the insides which were pinkish and white. And that was not all her anal area was now an exposed cavity about a foot in width, her entrails, stomach, everything within, had been removed. The scarring around both wounds was clean and blood-free as though opened and sealed with a surgical laser. What remained of her tail was a stub of about six inches perfectly sliced, in two. The remainder lay next to the body; some was matted with mud appearing to have been stepped on at one point. The lack of blood in and around the corpse indicated obvious signs of excision. I made it a point to examine the stored photographs just to make sure they were saved properly. I had no idea what to do with them momentarily but I planned on doing some research when I got home.

Through the years I had looked through websites that featured cattle mutilations in America and from around the world but, I had never expected to find a mutilation. As I stood there with the sun fully warming my side of the world I felt so insignificant, small and fearful. A feeling of being watched imperceptibly entered my spirit, and my body began to gently shake. The sensation grew and I rushed to my car, slowly drove away and looked one last time at the poor creature not wanting to leave her but needing to get away just the same.

Now I regret not having had sense enough to have taken photos of the UFO when I first saw it, the tie-in to the mutilation would have been sensational and undoubtedly would have caused much controversy.

I should not have been stupid enough however, to have returned to the site. Now I'm in hiding not having expected what was to come.

Chapter Two

The day after I found the mutilation I decided to go back out of plain curiosity. The afternoon, was warm and beautifully sunny, the sky was a brilliant and crystal blue providing me with wonder and a false sense of strength.

The mare's corpse was gone.

Surprised, I looked around to see if it was the correct location, not being sure as it had been dark the morning before. Walking around I saw familiar landmarks and finally found the depression on the ground left by the horse's weight. A small amount of blood with three large bubbles had pooled in a tiny depression in the soil. This time I was prepared with camera in hand and took pictures of the area. As I reviewed the photos just as before, my eyes were drawn to a small but brilliant item in one picture. I almost walked away before deciding to return and see just what that was.

The strength I'd felt earlier drained from my body the second I set eyes on the implement. Kneeling, I touched its surface which felt cool, although it had been sitting in the sun all day. It appeared brand new, whatever this odd-looking thing was. I called it an implement because it had an appearance of a tool, a fine one at that. Its surface seemed to draw and reflect the sun and glow at the same time, one edge was extremely sharp like a scalpel, the other side was blunt with two rounded edges, the other end singular also round, the blunt edge glowed brighter as though a light were inside it and felt as though it belonged in my hand. It felt, comfortable, it made me feel...*good*.

The tool began to vibrate softly, glow brighter and let out a gentle hum as I held it, dropping it in fear I stepped away looking all around and above me. Why had I also looked up? I felt as though I were being watched again, except this time from above.

I returned to my car and sat inside for a long time until I felt calm again. Not wanting fear to drive me away and leave the implement behind, I forced myself to retrieve it. In the trunk, I carry a pair of rubber gloves which come in handy when washing my car, or changing a tire, wearing them I cautiously lifted the tool and stood motionless not feeling a thing. For reasons unknown, I no longer felt spied on. Tossing the tool in the glove compartment and feeling a tiny bit apprehensive, I started the car up and fainted.

Chapter Three

I dreamt with visions of stars and then an expansive extreme darkness overwhelmed my mind, a rush of energy sent tremors through my slumbering body which caused me to open my eyes, only to find myself nude on a black slab of a table. Unable to move, tears of unmitigated fright rolled off my face and sizzled on the surface below although I saw the steam, amazingly I felt no heat against my body. I was somehow held down as though by a magnet. To my right an image approached, it moved as though gliding through the air. As it neared, a strong surge of fright overcame me and I screamed loudly. The terror ran through and through shaking me fiercely. The horrible and terrifying near reality made me piss and shit on the slab. The steam from both entered my nostrils causing nausea and even more fear. Even though I was literally free of restraints I could not rise nor run off. My exhausted body trembled and whimpered like a sickly speechless beast.

Suddenly I awoke and found myself in my car, sitting on a pile of my own filth.

The night air slammed against my face as I leaned out of the window driving rapidly through traffic, needing to find a restroom or port-a-potty in which to remove my pants and clean myself. I felt shame and cried uncontrollably as I rushed past restaurants and red lights. A police car fired up its lights and siren and desperately drove fast after me. Finally, he called out to me ordering me to stop immediately over the loudspeaker. I did so and as he approached with gun drawn he ordered me out of my vehicle with my hands showing. I didn't move as fast as he wished so he charged up to me and pointed his weapon at my reddened face. He suddenly stopped and drew back overpowered by the reeking stench emanating from my car. He looked with disgust at my tear swollen face and began to laugh aloud. My voice was like that of a child crying for forgiveness. He shook his head looking away while mumbling something about worst case of diarrhea and waved me off, not wanting me near his patrol car much less inside. I slowly drove away and decided to go home, no longer caring about cleaning myself before getting there.

At home, I made my way to the side of the house where the garden hose is stored and removed my clothes hosing them down before dumping them in the trash can along the path. I rinsed off with cold water not caring how it felt against my already traumatized body.

Chapter Four

I stayed in bed for two days which were a Monday and Tuesday, my boss had been kind enough to allow me the remainder of the week off as well, I claimed a death in the family and she didn't question me further. Somehow saying that, made me realize that the person I'd once been no longer existed and I had experienced a renewal or birthing of some kind which made me feel different, whole...

I held the implement in my gloved hands turning it this way and that, fascinated by both its beauty and the mystery it held, while sitting under the covers of my bed. A feeling of unbridled childhood returned to my soul while playing pretend with it, marveling at its exquisite form and marvelous glow. The feeling of possessing something so odd was refreshing and somewhat frightening. My fingers yearned to touch it but remembering the fainting spell and the terrifying dream kept me from doing so. After two days of playing under the covers, I realized that I hadn't eaten or taken a drink and had not felt the urge to do so either. My hand trembled as I peeked out from below the covers, the room was engulfed in darkness and if it weren't for the soft glow of the tool, I would not have seen. Reaching out to turn the lamp switch on, I realized that the air in the room had grown cold. Not cool, but breath floating from my mouth cold. Although it was summer I hadn't turned the AC on for days making me wonder just what the hell was happening.

I finally made it out of bed, turned the heater on and headed to the bathroom where I bathed in a steaming shower until the hot water began running cool. Afterwards I dressed, ate breakfast and saw that the time was six in the evening not morning as I had thought. Looking out through my bedroom window I noticed a red glow illuminating my backyard, a chill ran through me and I suddenly grew angry, realizing that I'd been experiencing fear now for days and I'd never in my life felt so much fright for such an extended time. Sliding the door open, I walked out into the yard and the red glow disappeared before my eyes. Looking up I noticed that a patch of darkness covered a section of the sky obliterating the stars. As I tried making out the silhouette a sudden ray of bright blue light came down freezing me in place. Just as quickly, the ray of light drew back and the dark spot illuminated itself in a dull hue of yellow/orange and rapidly shot off into the darkness. I looked across the yard and saw my neighbor staring at me in shock, cigarette in his mouth and a match burning the redwood patio floor by his foot. He didn't move for a while and when he did, he stomped down on the match, spun around and rushed inside his home. I hadn't met my neighbor and had only on occasion waved to him and his wife whenever I did happen to see them sitting and smoking enjoying a quiet break outdoors. Now I wondered if he'd ever approach me or just stare from a distance.

I felt as though I'd been violated and that pissed me off!

I didn't know what to do but felt a need to do something. Where could I go for help? Who would want to get involved? To whom could I turn? I sat and stared at my PC for a while before typing out: *Does anyone know who or what can help when attacked by...*by what??? Refocusing, I finished by adding the word *extraterrestrials.*

A list of websites suddenly appeared all having something to do with ET's but only one came up offering resistance through prayer and something called an orgone device, not much help there.

I sat on the couch with all lights in the house turned on.

Chapter Five

The mall parking lot was full of cars but I could only see one other person walking away from me about three lanes distant. The night was quiet, the only sounds were coming from the buzzing of the lights illuminating the immediate area and the distant sound of cars whizzing by on the freeway about a half mile from where I stood. I'd been in the house for days and since I didn't have family in town to visit or invite over, I decided to go out. My mind was on the movie I'd read about and was preparing to watch when something caught my attention out of the corner of my eye. Something was walking towards me from between the cars and it seemed to hobble as it approached, oddly enough, it appeared to be wearing a thin transparent raincoat. My curiosity kept me rooted to the spot and as it neared the light I could see it had a large head and a small humanlike body with arms extending unnaturally near its knees. Whatever it was, it kept a steady pace but fear started to build in me so, I turned my head and hurried towards the mall entrance. I could feel it coming up behind me as I quickened my pace not wanting to run but not wanting it to get close either. My heart began beating faster and a panic started to well up in me. For no reason at all I suddenly stopped and spun around to confront whatever it was that followed, but nothing was there. Confused and wondering what had just happened I looked around once more and again found nothing. People began exiting the mall, obviously, a movie had just ended and I began to feel a little better.

I paid for the movie and waited to hear the commercials and previews before going in.

Don't ask me what the movie was about, I fell asleep at the beginning credits and a young kid wearing a vest and tie woke me up so he could clean the aisle.

When I walked out, the lot was empty except for my car which sat lonely out in the middle of nowhere. I looked at it like a survivor on a life raft seeing an approaching island with a little fear and trepidation plus a sense of joy and relief. Being the only one in the darkness, I looked around and mustered the courage to look up into the dark night sky before running as fast as I could to my waiting island.

The car was my refuge, going through a variety of events with me in its driver's seat, thus giving me a sense of comfort. I straightened myself in the seat and buckled myself in, placed the key in the ignition and turned it. Nothing happened.

I sat there frozen with surprise and tried again. Nothing, not a single click, I looked out through my windshield to an empty lot. I pulled out my cell phone and it was dead. I sat there for minutes feeling helpless. Just then, a pair of lights turned into the lot and headed towards me. For a second I wondered if they knew I was in trouble, but how was that possible? The lights kept coming towards me, I reached for the door handle when I looked up the lights were above the hood. A blue light suddenly enveloped my car and I froze in fear, I gently closed my eyes not wanting to see what was next.

My clothes were on the floor before me. I stood, somehow restrained to a flat metallic board that I could feel against my back and ass, it felt cold. A pair of figures resembling the oddity I'd seen in the mall parking lot stood a few feet away, their backs to me. They were communicating with each other and appeared to be examining something that glowed in the hands of one. As one separated slightly from the other I was shocked to see the implement. I couldn't move or scream as the one holding the implement came towards me. The board suddenly fell backwards shocking me further. The creature placed its face close to my chest and pressed the implement against it. I couldn't feel a thing. I couldn't move but I was shaking with fright inside my skin. My eyes closed of their own accord.

I awoke in my car it was running quietly, my cell phone lay next to me, the time was eight minutes after three. I rubbed my chest on the very spot where the implement had touched me and could feel a small bump beneath the skin. I also felt another on my neck just above the collar and to the left of my spine. My nose trickled blood. I sat in my car and cried for a long time.

Chapter Six

My hands shake uncontrollably as I place the pistol to my left temple. I've decided not to be an experiment anymore. Not knowing where and when I'll be in their hands again is too overwhelmingly frightening. I'm no longer in control of my destiny, I can barely think straight. I can't go on like this, I can't eat or sleep. I can't look in the mirror without seeing them.

I've written all of this down to the best of my recollection and ability. After my body is found, it won't matter anymore what becomes of it, but right now I am taking control and have decided what is best for me.

I hope that someday this thing that is obviously happening to others comes to a stop. I also pray that my family forgives me. They, whoever they are, did not put this pistol to my head, I have chosen to do this, no one has talked me into this, I've decided on my own.

This DVD is proof of what I have said and written, it serves as testimony to these last miserable weeks of my life. One more thing, if for some reason, I fuck this up and end up in a coma, please, please do not let anyone try to revive me or keep me on life support! Don't even think about plugging me in just to later decide to unplug me. Don't worry, just let me go.

I love all of you, always have and always will.

Chapter Seven

After receiving a call from a distraught couple in Chicago, who'd received a four- day old suicide letter from their son, the Houston Police Department sent a patrol unit to the home to investigate. Expecting a macabre and putrid scene, the patrol officers entered with faces covered only to discover no body. A note was on the couch along with a fully loaded 9mm semi-automatic pistol. No blood, no body.

The senior officer walked up to the television set and pressed the play button on the DVD player and was surprised to see a young man talking about suicide. He could see the note resting in the same place as when he first saw it, and the 9mm in the young man's shaking hand. Suddenly, a bright blue flash consumes the screen and just as quickly vanishes, the young man is no longer present, but the note remains on the couch, and the pistol which is now on the carpet, slowly falls to one side, the cushion no longer bearing weight slowly rises. Confused by what he has just witnessed, the officer replays the scene over and over, occasionally, looking at the timer to see if any time is missing. Convinced that there is no missing time, he shakes his head and removes the DVD from the player. His young partner, who has quietly watched the final minute of the recording after having first scoured the house, shakes his head also and turns to accompany his partner out of the empty house. They both wonder about the flash, not ever having seen such a bright and beautiful blue before.

END

BLACK SOUL

Chapter One

My name is Carl Gross. I'm a twin, my brother Kyle died at eighteen back in nineteen hundred and sixty-eight. I've decided to tell my well, *our* story after all these years because I want the truth to be told before I die so, others will know. I've agreed to be interviewed on video so, that people can see the scars on my face and body and know that it was because of hate that I got them and my brother, killed. Kyle was only eighteen back then in nineteen hundred and sixty-eight, like I said before. Anyways, here goes, I guess.

Carl: Do you want me to answer questions for you or, do you just want me to start at the start?

Videographer: No Sir, you can start where you wish and if we have any questions, we'll go from there. That ok?

Carl: Sure, that'll be fine. Well, my Daddy's name was Gunther Gross and his Daddy came from Germany many years ago. My Daddy and he went their separate ways when his Daddy decided to mess with a younger girl instead of staying with his wife, my Granma. My Granma took it hard and took her own life on her fiftieth birthday because of it. According to my Daddy, Granma was a beautiful girl when she was young and Grandpa stole her from her folks and never married her. I guess that's why he took on with the young girl, feeling like he had no marriage bond and all. He died in an automobile accident in Mississippi back in nineteen hundred and twenty-five I believe it was. I think I'm going too far back. I'd better stick to what I know instead of what I was told. Well, my Daddy Gunther hated anyone who wasn't a white man like himself. He was always quoting the Bible and telling everyone who'd listen, that Negroes were the sons of Lucifer and all niggers had to be separate from good Christian folk so that them there nigger men, wouldn't rape and steal our God fearing white women and girls. He knew they would take our lives if given a chance and then run off with our women folk. If a Negro was walking on the street and he looked up at us my Daddy Gunther would not hesitate to beat'im with his cane till that boy would run off crying and wailing, if he was lucky. Daddy Gunther was a mean son of a bitch. I don't want to sound disrespectful and all that but, he was a bastard. When we were little boys, about eight years old, he took Kyle and me to a lynching. I know that sounds harsh and all, but that was life back then. He made us stand next to the hanging and told us to smile for the cameraman. I don't know what happened to that picture of us, I only saw it once or twice before Daddy was killed. I was already burned and Kyle was already dead when Daddy died. I was twenty-three then. He took to drinking heavy after the accident and never forgave himself for what happened to us in '68. He was only fifty-three but looked sixty something all gray haired, tired and haggard looking, walking all crouched and everything. He'd lost his cane by then and never did replace it with another. I gave him one but he didn't like it, I guess cause, he never used it. One day, in Pasadena Texas he walked into a bar and started quoting scripture to a bunch of tired drunks and they didn't want to hear none of it. A couple of them boys got up and carried him to the door and threw him out face first. He was nearly a cripple you know, and when he hit the gravel well, it wasn't a good thing. Daddy Gunther got up, dusted himself off and hobbled back into that bar. With the Bible in one hand and a straight razor in the other, he went after those boys but they were too big and mean for his scrawny old self. One boy knocked him down with a punch to the face and the other kicked him a few times in the ribs. That's all it took for Daddy to die a few hours later in the back alley of that old bar where they tossed him. No one reported the murder and his body was found a couple of days later by a hobo, who stopped a police car. No one cared that he was killed or that he even lived once. I found out about it at the hospital where I was still being helped five years later for my burns.

It was about then that I met Sally. She was a nurse and all and looked about sixteen but she said she was twenty-seven. That surprised the hell out of me! She'd worked with soldiers, burn victims being treated at a VA hospital, so she had experience and wasn't scared to touch me. I was scared and hurting trying to move my arms a bit better. I'd lost most of my face in the fire. I don't have ears and only three fingers on my right hand and two on my left. I always kept my head down during those times, I didn't want to scare nobody. None of the other lady nurses really looked at me, any time they asked me questions, they'd look off to the side as though talking to someone next to me. Only the old battle-axes would touch my arms, but never my face. I guess they'd seen plenty in their years. I remember Sally holding my hand the first time and I nearly jumped when I realized it. She held me tight and looked into my eyes and didn't wince or look away. She had tears in her eyes after I told her how Kyle died and I was burned trying to save him. I need to stop for a minute or two.

One hour later:

Carl: I guess I'd better tell you about the accident now.

Kyle'd been working at the local filling station all day. He'd wanted to be a mechanic since we were little. He collected all kinds of toy cars and trucks. I collected fishing tackle, no toys for me! Daddy Gunther collected followers. He also followed, though. He belonged to the Klan ever since he was a teenager in Mississippi. Grandpa Gross was not a leader but he led a group of young men who belonged to a larger clan there in Mississippi. Daddy Gunther got in trouble with a woman who was married to a Klansman. He was caught with her out in a field, you know? They'd been out doing their ahhhh, their lovemaking. I guess you'd call it? The man's eldest son seen'em and went and told his daddy. The man went out with a shotgun and chased them around the fields. He shot at but missed Daddy Gunther and hit the woman in the leg. Daddy Gunther brought us to Houston right after.

We'd been living near Pasadena and Daddy heard of a Klan there about so, he went around asking about it. He was let in after a while.

I don't know how or with whom, he joined. He didn't talk about it much. I guess he could see that the future was going to change and we'd be different somehow. The government was making changes and America was going to change whether the Klan liked it or not. Daddy Gunther didn't like the government telling him what to do, but he knew things would change eventually. He grew angrier and angrier the more things did change. When he heard about Martin Luther King making speeches in public telling the government to change things, he'd spit and curse and get to drinking. He wanted us to hate Negroes as much as he did.

Damn, I'm rambling. Let me get back to the accident. Daddy Gunther stopped by the service station that afternoon and told Kyle to come get me from the bayou I'd gone fishing to and join him at a chapel not far from the house. He said he had something important to tell us and we'd better get there as soon as possible. When Kyle picked me up he looked nervous. I asked him why he looked scared and he told me that he'd heard a customer tell the station manager that the Klan was going to burn down a nigger's house tonight and he thought Daddy Gunther was involved and he'd probably ask us to help him. See, Daddy asked Kyle to bring along two five-gallon cans of gasoline with us. Kyle was driving an old pick-up and the cans were in the back. I'd thrown my rod and reel in the back and saw them there. I asked Kyle why Daddy wanted to do such a thing and he said that probably the Klan was testing him. I guess Kyle knew more about that than I did cause, I was usually to myself and he was working and meeting people. By the way, he was getting good at being a mechanic. He just loved getting greasy and dirty working on those cars people brought to the station. I preferred being clean. I wasn't lazy, you know? I just didn't like being dirty.

When we got to the chapel, Daddy was on his knees praying. I don't know what he was praying about but he sure looked worried as he knelt there shaking and shivering like it was cold in the middle of summer. After a few minutes, he got up and put his arms on our shoulders and started talking in a whisper. There was nobody there with us but he whispered like he didn't want anyone to hear. Daddy told us that he was ordered to burn out a family of niggers that had moved into a white neighborhood that didn't want them there. It was his duty to do what he'd been asked and he wanted us to help him do it. He told us that it was our duty to protect the family and his friends from those nigger devils. He talked about all kinds of things the government was planning to do and one was to integrate the schools and neighborhoods all over the country. He kept saying that he was stupid for messing up in Mississippi and how he wished we could go back cause, he knew things would take a lot longer to make those changes the government was going to make. Anyway, we had to listen to him wail and complain for a couple of hours till it grew dark. I didn't like that he was asking us to help him. I asked Daddy, why his Klan friends couldn't help him instead. He nearly slapped me and yelled at me calling me a coward. I grew angry but he didn't give a damn what I thought. He said we had to do it and that was that. Since Daddy didn't have a car, Kyle had to drive us to the house, which was set pretty far back from the street and surrounded by large oak trees. Before we got there, we stopped by an old farmhouse and picked up some shovels and a white seven-foot cross that we had to plant, or erect, I mean, and burn it along with the house. Tell you the truth, I was scared as hell. I kept looking around as we drove looking to make sure no one could see what we were up to. Every car that went by I just curled up and slinked down between Kyle and Daddy Gunther. Daddy himself was scared but did his best not to show it once we got in the truck. He smelled of liquor and I knew that without it, he wouldn't have the courage to do anything like what we now had to do. Kyle looked all calm and collected he never ever seemed to worry about a thing. He was the most courageous person I knew. I don't think he wanted to follow Daddy's orders, he just knew he had no say in the matter just like me. Well, we drove around the streets seeing as to who was home and what not. No one seemed to be in the big house when we drove by a few times so, it looked safe enough. Kyle and I carried the cross and shovels and quickly dug a hole and stood the cross up as best we could. It was dark by then. Daddy brought along the gas cans and began soaking the cross. He hurriedly handed over a can to Kyle and sloshed him with some gasoline. Kyle was wearing his dirty coveralls which were already soaked with oil and grease. He took out a rag and wiped his hands and face where the gas hit him and put the rag in a back pocket. We both ran to the front porch and I began emptying the other can on the railing and steps and ran the entire wrap around porch sloshing gasoline on the doors and windows.

Daddy Gunther in the meantime was keeping an eye out on the streets and yelled out when he saw a car coming. We ducked behind the railing until the car drove past and then Kyle and I ran into each other. My can fell and Kyle's was already empty so he threw it through one of the windows. That's when we both heard a scream. We stopped and looked at each other for a moment, then we both jumped off the porch and ran to Daddy who had just lit a rag on fire he'd tied to a stick. When Kyle bumped into Daddy he almost knocked him down so he grabbed Daddy by the arm and brought that flaming rag against his shoulder. It all happened so fast, Kyle's overalls caught fire in what sounded like a huge, whoosh! Daddy jumped back in fright and I knocked Kyle to the ground. My shirt then caught fire too. We rolled around the ground stuck to each other until Daddy kicked at us to separate us. I fainted and don't know what happened after that. Daddy told me months later that Kyle's overalls which were already covered in oil and grease couldn't be put out. He died right there on the lawn under those tall oak trees. Daddy Gunther was arrested and put in jail for months. I didn't see him for about eleven months until he was escorted in handcuffs to the hospital by a deputy sheriff to pay me a visit. He told me that he'd pleaded with a judge to let him come see me. The judge, he told me years later, was a friend of the Klan. Daddy wept like a child when he saw me all wrapped up and cried even more when he realized he couldn't hug me. He stood near my legs and feet and pressed against my hip once before he was taken away. The judge later on let him out of jail and fined him a small amount for damages to the property.

The Klan didn't want anything to do with him afterwards. I guess they didn't want to be associated with a screw-up. Daddy never forgave them for that. While I was going through therapy, Daddy only visited me once and told me he'd sent Kyle's body back to Mississippi. He was going to go bury him and would come back as soon as he had enough money to come back.

I need a break. I've got to change shirts. I've been drooling on this one. Sorry about that! I can't control the drooling, just like I can't tear up. I got no tear ducts, you see.

The next day

Videographer: Mr. Gross, would you mind telling us about the time of your rehabilitation?

Carl: Well, I can't tell you about that time without telling you about Sally. Remember her? She was a nurse who helped me more than anybody

Videographer: Of course. You can say whatever comes to mind, please.

Carl: Thanks son. It was a difficult time to say the least. I'd never known what true pain was until then. Sure, I'd stuck hooks into my hand and thumb before and it hurt like hell pulling out a treble hook once, but that was nothing compared with burns. Imagine, I couldn't blink my eyes; they couldn't ever tear up again. My lips were gone and I drool even now. I look like a monster to others and back then, I couldn't look at my reflection especially a mirror. My hands had stumps instead of fingers and my arms, chest and stomach looked like, beat up leather. At night when mostly everyone was asleep, I was awake so, that I could sleep during the day and not have to answer people's questions. So, therapy was very difficult and extremely painful. No matter how much I tried, I couldn't help but yell out when I hurt, and that was most of the time!

I didn't hear or see Daddy Gunther for a couple of years. I used to think and sometimes pray that, maybe he was killed by that man whose wife he'd messed with back home. In the meantime, I suffered and suffered through all the therapy. Then, Nurse Sally Wells appeared. She was different from all the other nurses. Sally actually cared about her patients. She was after your heart like those other nurses were after doctors. She was the only nurse who would look at me in the eyes. She would touch my chin and raise my head up so that I had no choice but to look into her eyes. I couldn't shut mine, you know?

Sally made me laugh again. Look, can we stop for a moment?

Two hours later:

Videographer: Sir, are you about ready? I've got to leave early today. My girl and I are celebrating her birthday with dinner tonight.

Carl: Sure, son. Give me a moment to sit properly. I was released from the hospital some time later. It was nearly two years, I believe. I thought I'd never see Sally again and I was scared, broke and angry. The state gave me a place to live and a little bit of money to survive on. All those years my Daddy hated the government and here it was serving me. Wasn't that funny how things worked out? After a few days of being alone and not wanting to go out into the world, Sally came knocking on my door. At first, I ignored the knocking, I just didn't want to be seen. But, she kept knocking and kicking and finally called out my name. I rushed to the door then and came up with some bullshit that I was on the toilet or something. She didn't believe me from the look on her face but she smiled and started talking like we'd been talking all day. She had brought along some groceries and cleaned up the kitchen and cooked while doing that. I felt like a little kid, unable to move or talk much. Sally just kept it up until we sat down to eat. She laughed when some food fell out of my mouth and fork and told me I looked like a fish out of water. That made me smile and embarrassed me at the same time. She had a way of doing that. Sally smiled all the time and reminded me of Kyle in that, nothing seemed to bother her. She was strong willed and soft hearted. She made me forget about my scars sometimes and I almost felt like the world was ok again.

Since she came by just about every day, I finally drummed up the courage to ask her about *her* life. She grew quiet and serious and I felt that she'd probably start crying and then leave. I told her I was sorry for prying and she didn't have to answer. A couple of minutes went by like, she was drawing up strength to talk about herself. For the first time, she wasn't looking right at me when she spoke, and when she did, she sounded like a little girl. "My brothers raped me when I was nine," she said. I wanted her to stop right then but I couldn't talk. "I have two brothers and an older sister. My mother worked at a cleaner's and stayed late making overtime almost every day that she worked. My sister was out doing things she wasn't supposed to do, earning money any way she could, so she was hardly ever around the house. I mostly read and played with my dolls, hardly ever leaving my room except to eat and go to the toilet. I don't know why or how my brothers got the idea to do what they did but they came to my room and started playing dolls with me. It was so much fun cause, being boys they hardly payed me any mind. Well, they began to play doctor with me and took off their clothes and then took mine off too. I don't know what I was thinking except that it was fun to be naked and my brothers not laugh at me. They began to touch me and when I started to feel like something was wrong, they sensed it and tied me up. They covered my mouth with my pillow and then, then they raped me."

I wanted to cry and beat her brothers just then. I wanted her to stop. My heart couldn't take it. For the first time in my life, I wanted to kill someone! How could they do that to her? Her own brothers? Sally cried and sat there for a long time. I didn't want to move, thinking if I did, she'd leave right away! Slowly, I reached out and touched her hands. She was holding them on her lap like, she was praying. She didn't take her hands away and I felt better. I don't know why I did it, but I slowly dropped to my knees and lay my head on her hands and lap. Sally placed her hands on my head and suddenly I felt ... love. At least that was the only way I could describe what I felt then.

Ok, then! Let's stop here so, you can take your girl out and celebrate. Ok?

Chapter Two

Videographer: Good morning Mr. Gross. I hope you're well today. Ready to get started?

Carl: Morning son. Yeah, I guess I'm ready. Would you like a cup of coffee first?

Videographer: No, thank you, Sir. I had one earlier.

Carl: Do me a favor, ok? Call me Carl, ok?

Videographer: Alright, Carl. Thank you.

Carl: I was telling you about Sally Wells yesterday. I want to talk about her just a bit more, if you don't mind. I didn't see Sally for a couple of days after our last lunch and I started to panic. I thought that she was probably embarrassed about what she'd told me and decided not to come back. I felt trapped in that little apartment. I wanted to go looking for her, but I didn't know where to look. I didn't have an address, or a phone number. I was afraid to call the rehab place or the hospital to ask about her. I didn't want to jeopardize her job, you see. Three days later, she came right through the front door like she lived there and dumped two bags of groceries on the table. She took off her jacket, took my hand and led me to the kitchen table.

"Carl, I hope that I didn't make a fool of myself the other day. I suppose I needed to get that off my chest and it seemed the proper time and you seemed to be the proper person to hear it. Please forgive me."

I was so, happy that I couldn't talk. I took her hands and held them tightly. Then, when I could talk, I told her that I was both sad about what had happened to her and glad that she'd confided in me. I told her how much I had missed her company and how I felt scared that she might not come back. Sally, took her hands, cupped my chin with them and then kissed me. I shook like a frightened puppy! I didn't know what to do. My eyes couldn't stop looking at hers and she never once looked away. That feeling I'd had before, came back like a wave, engulfing me. I felt like I was drowning. Sally pushed her chair back then got on her knees and lay her head on my lap. I could only rest my head on hers. Her hair smelled of perfumed shampoo and it was the best scent I had ever smelled in my life. Her head was warm and I wished I could cry.

Videographer: Carl? Do you have any tissues? I'm sorry! I mean, I need tissues. I'll go to the bathroom and take some toilet paper. I, um. I'll be right back. The camera is rolling, so you can keep talking if you wish. I'll hurry.

Carl: I had never been with a girl or woman before. Sally did everything to make me feel calm and comfortable. I had no idea what to do. She treated me as gently as one would hold a baby, I suppose. I never could have imagined what we did. I had thought about it when I was a teenager, but after the accident, I thought it would never happen. We made love and I felt so many things go through my head and my body. Yes, I felt pain too, but everything else erased it right away. Sally spent the night and cleaned me up and even took a shower with me. I was a bit embarrassed while showering yet, it seemed so natural to her. I couldn't believe that she could look at me and my scars and not be repulsed. Every time I began to say something about it, she would shush me and hold me tightly. It worked, as I never mentioned it again, ever. Sally meant the world to me, and more!

One day, she announces that she was moving out of her apartment and wondered if, I would accept her as my roommate. I was floored! Stunned! I shouted. Yes! Before I knew it, we were living together. I had never been happier. I don't believe I've ever been as happy. We loved one another deeply. Anything she asked of me, I'd do without question. She took me out of the apartment for the first time and into the community. I couldn't believe that she had made me courageous enough not to give a damn what people thought of me and my scars or of us together. I felt like I could do anything because of her. I loved her, so much.

We were eating dinner one evening when someone knocked on our door. I went over opened the door and there stooped and smelling of booze was, Daddy Gunther. He looked at me for minute, began to cry and hugged me tightly. I stood there shocked and stiff as a board. He looked at me again and asked if he could come in. For a fraction of a second, I didn't move. I didn't want him to come in and yet, felt obligated to let him in. We stood in the living area and he started to apologize for taking so long to look me up and asked at the hospital about me. Sally walked up behind me and asked what was going on. Daddy Gunther's eyes grew as big as saucers. *What's this nigger girl doing here? Who the hell is she, the maid?* Sally was shocked to hear the old man talking shit and yelled at him to get the hell out of our home. Daddy looked at me with so much anger that he spits on our floor and ran for the door, slamming it on his way out. I turned around and hugged Sally as tightly as I could. Then I had to explain that the old man was my father.

"Why would he call me a nigger girl?" she asked. It took me all night practically, to tell her about Daddy Gunther and of course I had to explain the circumstances of the accident and Kyle's death and so on. Sally didn't talk to me for a full day and I felt I'd lost her for sure. My heart was in so much pain that I couldn't talk without choking up. In bed the next evening, she turned away from me for the very first time and I wanted to just die right then and there. All night I couldn't sleep but I didn't want to move either. I felt trapped again, like before. When Sally finally awoke, she turned around and kissed my cheek. She sat up and asked me to forgive her anger. I hugged her waist and asked her to forgive all the anger and wrongs I had ever committed because of the bad things that were taught me. She told me that she'd never been called a "nigger" to her face; that had hurt her the most. I begged her to forgive my past again and again. I swore that I would never go back to that black soul I had been when I was young and stupid. She smiled and held me too. Sally was the most forgiving human being. Later that same day, she told me that if my father wanted to see or talk to me again, he was welcome in our house. I wished I could cry. I held her in my arms and never wanted to let go.

Her anger was gone before Daddy Gunther made an appearance. He knocked softly on the door and asked Sally politely, if he could speak to me. Sally reached out, took his skinny arm and pulled him inside. Daddy Gunther sat before his cup of coffee and quietly cried. He wiped his nose on his sleeve until Sally brought him a roll of tissue. He thanked her and slowly began to apologize to Sally and then me. He asked us to please forgive him and promised never to say, "Nigger, "again. Then he apologized for saying it that time too. It was hard on both of them but after a year of getting to know one another, they found a mutual respect. Daddy Gunther ended up loving my Sally, too!

What I'm going to talk about now is going to be tough for me, so bear that in mind as I tell it.

Sally came home from work one day and asked me to sit down and have some tea. I knew right away something was wrong. She smiled the biggest smile and told me that she'd gone to see a friend of hers who was also a nurse who worked for a Pediatrician. Right away, the friend asked her how many months she was pregnant and Sally laughed. The friend was serious. Sally was seen by the doctor and she confirmed Sally's pregnancy. She couldn't believe it and had to come tell me right away. I hugged and kissed her for a long, long time. Daddy Gunther took the news a bit hard at first but then he was happy for us and for himself as he was going to be a Grandpa!

Sally's belly was growing a nice little hump and I'd hold and kiss it as often as I could.

Grandpa Gunther started carving wooden toys like an old sailor or puppeteer. He was finally a happy man. One day, he left a tiny wooden duck on Sally's pillow and she placed it in her purse for safe keeping that morning. His small display of love for our baby, I suppose. After breakfast she asked if I'd go with her to see the doctor and I quickly dressed.

When the doctor came out to see us, he asked us if we had insurance. We looked at each other and shook our heads, no. He asked us to follow him to his office so we could talk privately. I was hoping he'd give us a way to make payments for the delivery and any medical bills. Before I could ask, I heard the word, cancer. I was dumbstruck. What is he talking about? I asked myself. Sally was already in tears. We left his office and went home to what was once a happy home. The whole time we were in the doctor's office, I went numb and deaf. Sally had to explain everything all over. Two months? Two months is what he said? Grandpa Gunther snuffled when we told him, he walked out.

I, I'm getting choked up, son. I want to stop but don't have much more to say. Give me a minute.

Videographer: Take your time, Carl. I'll be right back!

Fifteen minutes later:

Carl: Sally was the best and I mean *"The Best,"* thing that ever happened to me, ever. There is nothing to compare. Absolutely, nothing! If it wasn't for her love, I'd never have known it. You know what, son? That old adage, "Love conquers all?" It's true, it's true. Sally Wells died one morning in our bed and in my arms, where she always wanted to be. We lost the baby before she passed, of course. And, she didn't die in two months like the doctor predicted. She left us in five weeks. I've never married and I never will. After Grandpa Gunther was killed, I decided to move to a new apartment. I couldn't live where my Sally died. It was too much for me. Well, now I've got cancer. Isn't that a charm? I have maybe a month left. The pain is not as bad as my burns but it's painful. I refuse chemotherapy. What do I have to live for anyway? My Sally and our baby are waiting for me. Grandpa Gunther and Kyle are waiting too! I can't wait to see them again. Love, love is what we need, son. Nothing else. Absolutely, nothing else.

Videographer: Shuts off the camera...

END

THE EXORCISM

The conflagration which had turned his home into ash was purposely lit. Upon seeing the devastation, Carlo smiled broadly.

The blue sky and luminous sun gave the day a fresh start; for days, rains had befallen the bedroom community for over a week. Young joggers, fast walkers and dogs on leashes resumed their regular routines. School buses delivered their charges according to schedule and all was back to the normalcy everyone typically assumed without much thought.

Carlo Bono was a small rotund man with a Spanish accent, assumed with his many years of experience living in Mexican cities beginning fresh out of college. He was the youngest of his family and his father Carlo Sr., who had been a strict disciplinarian from first born to last, had given Carlo reason to escape home to seek exotic places. He'd studied primitive people and their cultures since childhood, becoming an ethnologist much to the chagrin of his father. The elder Carlo expected all his sons to follow, like himself, the lucrative practice of law. He cared little for the education of his daughters, he expected they marry into wealthy families and follow their husbands' wise rule. His harsh behavior towards young Carlo was tempered with the fact that he harbored a deeper affection for the boy than he had ever felt for the older twins who reminded him more of their mother while the lovely plump child reminded him more of himself. The chubby boy had grown to disappoint, causing a rift within the family. Carlo Sr. had reluctantly paid his son's tuition praying in the family church to all the saints every morning before work, that the boy come to his senses and study law. When Carlo graduated with honors, Carlo Sr. shook his hand slightly and turned his back for good.

Carlo sat on a rock outcropping quietly napping as the shaman slowly neared. The healer was a tiny stooped figure dressed in the traditional cloth of the Huichol a native people of Mexico.

The holy man sat next to Carlo and smiled as he patiently waited for the rotund figure to awaken. The anthropologist awoke with a start, quickly wiping away the droll that had slipped past his pink fat lips onto his chin. He smiled excitedly as the old man eyed him intently. The old shaman was well known in the jungles and small towns in Mexico and had developed a reputation for curing ailments and divining accurately through many decades. No one knew his age, not even he. A story of his birth had preceded him throughout his life, the story was told that when he was birthed he opened his eyes and spoke three words in Nahuatl, "I am returned." His father took the newborn into the dense jungle, leaving him in the elements for three days. Upon returning, he discovered his son in the care and guard of a huge black jaguar. The animal growled as the father approached remaining still as the boy was lifted into his father's arms. As the father walked away from the spot, he turned to thank the jaguar which had silently vanished. Small globs of feces suddenly fell from above falling about the child's head causing it to cry out in shock. His father looked up to see a large bird directly above them, it was the Cara Cara, native eagle of Mexico, perched on a branch with wings spread apart staring down at the pair. A large feather slowly glided through the air to settle on the babe. The father thanked the eagle for blessing his child, giving it additional protection in unison with his friend Jaguar. The boy was pronounced "Winged Jaguar," without hesitation.

Carlo spoke enough Nahuatl to impress the shaman who was no longer hesitant to share a bit of knowledge with the smiling fat man. He took Carlo's hands and looked them over, he stared deeply into his eyes as well and then spit on the ground between them. Carlo had never heard of this behavior and asked the healer its meaning. The wizened man laughed profusely, relating that a gnat had entered a nostril and had to be expelled unfortunately, it happened while they embraced. Carlo burst out in laughter as they both clapped each other's backs. They took a seat on the ground and spoke without interpreter until Carlo ran out of words and needed assistance.

Javier his interpreter, was Mayan. He'd studied English at university and was quite versed in several native dialects. Carlo had met him in a nightclub one evening after having been invited for a night out by a group of archeologists he'd met previously. Javier was invited to the table by a mutual friend who suggested Carlo hire him in his forays into the jungle.

Javier was extremely happy to accept Carlo's offer of employ and joined him on this trip to meet Winged Jaguar, whom he had heard of but had never met. Winged Jaguar himself had invited Carlo to a spirit cleansing being held that evening at the home of a man who was apparently being visited by spirits who haunted his life mercilessly. Carlo warmly accepted the invitation, while Javier was reluctant. The wise man said something to Javier which Carlo could not hear. He waited for the shaman to depart before asking Javier, who refused to say, causing Carlo to grow petulant and wonder if he had made a mistake in hiring the man.

That evening they met at the home of the accursed villager forming a semi-circle in front of the man's hut. The old Shaman spoke quietly in prayer, lighting copal prior to walking around the dwelling allowing the smoke to slowly rise and fill the air. His associate, a young Indian man wiped the smoke gently with a bundle of feathers. Stopping outside the lone window. Winged Jaguar lifted the burning incense above his gray head then proceeded to the front and only entrance, slowly entering. The humble home with dirt floor and little furnishings allowed just enough room for the elderly couple who resided there and the four visitors who sat cross legged on the ground. The accursed man whose dark wide eyes stared intently at Winged Jaguar suddenly spit, hitting the shaman squarely on his nose. The shaman neither flinched nor wiped his face clean but instead continued praying. His voice muted and continued for some time. The young man made no effort to wipe the old man's face but instead retrieved items from a satchel and placed them in the burning bowl along with more copal. He would occasionally repeat some of the words prayed but not all. The villager in a low guttural voice began cursing at his visitors. His wife, a petite and round woman placed a caring hand on her husband's arm only to have it savagely bitten, causing her to scream in pain. Carlo and Javier quickly leapt to her defense only to have the young man hold them back. They hadn't noticed the man's restraints which held him firmly with rope until he began thrashing about, hissing and screaming at the top of his lungs. Carlo knew the vile words well, as they were the first he'd learned in Nahuatl. Feeling uncomfortable he rose to his knees with Javier's help and moved closer to the shaman and assistant. He wanted to hear the whispered prayers and found to his surprise that Winged Jaguar was praying in Latin! He was also versed to some degree in the ancient language and listened more intently. The villager shouted a Latin curse to the gathered! Carlo froze and scrutinized the contents of the abode, looking for any magazines, books, anything that would indicate an educated or knowledgeable man. He saw nothing of the sort not one book, nor radio not a television set, there was nothing there. Puzzled, he could only wait for answers. The accursed man smiled, stared intently at Carlo. In clear distinctive Italian and in Carlo senior's voice, he whispered, "Carlo! My beautiful bambino, I am here, my son." Carlo was stunned and fell back on his heels and haunches! Javier grabbed Carlo's arm and held him firmly as he watched the little fat man's tears run down his frightened face.

Winged Jaguar spit into the bowl of incense rubbing his thumb in the wet ash. He approached the wild man and carefully placed a large blotch on his forehead, pulling back just before the man lunged forward, howling and biting the air in rabid thrusts! The man quieted down after a time and the shaman continued to pray, this time in his native tongue with sprinklings of Spanish. Carlo sat back from the men, he was confused and could no longer look upon the villager, afraid to hear his father's voice once more. Javier saw the fright in Carlo's face and touched his shoulder as a way of showing support.

The young assistant looked over his shoulder at Carlo and smiled coyly. It appeared to Carlo that the man found the incident humorous, which angered him. For no good reason, Carlo lashed out and pushed the young man causing him to fall against the villager, who instantly bit the young man on the shoulder ripping his shirt and skin causing him to scream in pain as blood soaked through the white cotton shirt. The villager fell back on his bedding and passed out. The young assistant screamed a curse on Carlo and rushed at him in fierce anger! The Shaman now fell upon his assistant but was pushed away with great force. Javier also attempted to intercede but was easily pushed away. The young man threw himself onto Carlo who was rapidly crawling out of the hut. The man fell on his back and bit Carlo on the shoulder, just as he had been bitten. The Indio collapsed and fell heavily to the dirt floor. Carlo crawled outside fell on his back and screamed loudly to the sky and luminous stars. He held his shoulder and felt the blood as it soaked the khaki fabric. As he winced in pain he felt a pair of hands hold him firmly to the ground. It was Winged Jaguar who pinned him down with unbelievable strength. The Shaman attempted to place a dot of ash on Carlo's forehead but Carlo with incredible strength pushed him off, quickly jumping to his feet and stood in a protective stance. Javier who by now had recovered, stared at Carlo and laughed at seeing the chubby man behave like the soldiers he'd grown around as a child. He could not stifle the laughter and bent over holding his stomach in a foolish attempt to stop. Winged Jaguar's assistant exited the hut approached the Shaman and helped him to his feet. They all now stared at each other, not wanting to move or speak. The young man's shoulder still bled so the Shaman ripped his shirt open and began administering aid. Javier walked to Carlo and asked him to remove his shirt to look at the damage. Carlo retreated and would not permit his interpreter to touch him.

Javier turned and entered the hut. The old woman and husband hugged and silently wept in each other's arms. It appeared, as though the villager had recovered. Outside of the hut he approached the Shaman and the assistant who, appeared well, whatever the Shaman had used on the wound had stopped the bleeding. Carlo stood away in the darkness but Javier could hear his hard breathing and saw the glow of sweat in the starlight. He did not near him but instead shook the men's hands and departed into the jungle path to which they had arrived.

Winged Jaguar turned from his assistant and slowly approached Carlo who stood in silence. He said a Latin prayer and threw the contents of the bowl towards Carlo who jumped back and ran to the path disappearing into the black jungle.

Javier stood and stared at the vehicle he'd been brought in by Carlo. The doors were locked and he possessed no key. He sat against the front driver side tire and contemplated his position. After a few minutes he rose and began the long trek by foot, hoping not to encounter any beasts of the jungle. He hadn't walked far when he sensed and then heard something approaching from behind. He turned to look just in time to see Carlo coming at him at a great clip. Javier froze as he saw the little fat man move with great agility to jump at him. He only had time to lift his arms in defense before he felt Carlo bite his arms many times before fainting.

Carlo awoke to find himself prostrate on Javier's cold body. He recoiled upon seeing the blood covered corpse and fell backward upon the tall grass. His hands, arms and face were coated with Javier's dried blood. His khaki shirt was soaked and caked with blood and pieces of flesh. His mind spun as he tried to remember the events of the past evening. How would he explain the recent events to the authorities? Who would believe him? Where was Winged Jaguar and his assistant? How did things get out of hand? He began crying quietly until he could no longer hold back and screamed out in terror and disgust! Why did this happen? Why, him? He did not remember falling asleep and eventually stood on his trembling feet and legs. He walked to the SUV and found the keys dangling from the door's keyhole. Holding tightly to the key and turning it to the right, it automatically unlocked all doors. He searched through a duffel bag and found a clean shirt and pair of short pants which he put on after removing and folding his bloody clothes. He wanted to dispose of them as quickly as possible but did not want to do so in the jungle where they might eventually be discovered. He had taken Javier's body and dragged it into the dense jungle after locating a tree larger than most. Taking a shovel from the SUV he dug as much as he could and buried Javier in a shallow grave, placing plenty of foliage on top. Carlo believed that in a matter of a few days, the jungle animals would scatter the body about and eat most of it. He knew that insects would take care of the rest. For a while he contemplated crushing the skull and maybe cutting it off the corpse to bury farther off down the jungle road, he finally decided to leave the body intact and hoped for the best. He returned to the SUV and waited for nightfall before leaving the jungle for good. Rather than feeling fear and remorse, Carlo felt happy and stronger than he'd been feeling for years. His steps were lighter yet, he could not find it within him to smile. In fact, every time he glanced at his reflection in a mirror he barely recognized himself, he frowned so much. He stayed away from everyone retreating to his hotel room not responding to the telephone nor the knocks on the door. Carlo who was fastidious about cleanliness had forgotten to bathe and care for himself. He ordered little food from room service and ate even less. No one had come asking for Javier's whereabouts and he had not heard a word from Winged Jaguar or anyone including the police. Two fear-filled weeks passed before he decided to flee Mexico.

Upon returning to Italy Carlo discovered that his father had passed away the very evening he'd attended the cleansing which, as it had turned out been in fact, an exorcism. He'd been sleeping fitfully for days as ponderous nightmares racked his confused mind. He would see visions of creatures he'd never seen or read about. They would sometimes be friendly and at other times attack him. He lost much sleep and was in much need of rest but found none. Carlo bought over-the-counter medications to help him rest but found no relief. Fear of going to a doctor overwhelmed his senses so strongly that he could not get himself to do so. He found a slight sense of comfort only when lighting matches and fires in the huge chimney. Soon he found he could not allow the fire to go out. Carlo loved the warmth and the images he saw within the colorful flames as they leapt in large tongues that licked the cool air creating thin smoke which in turn formed creatures that smiled and laughed in delight. Carlo realized that the creatures were there for him! They were the creatures of his night terrors.

Carlo smiled as the smoke rose from the ashes of what had once been a beautiful two-story home. The firefighters walked around collecting their equipment, rolling the huge hoses and gathering in small groups. A fire chief walked up to Carlo to ask a few questions. The chief could not convince Carlo to speak, he walked away and chalked it up to shock. He'd send an assistant over in a few minutes as Carlo recovered.

"Carlo, my beautiful bambino, I am here, my son." he quietly repeated to himself over and over. "Carlo, my beautiful bambino, my beautiful bambino... Drool wet the sides of his mouth and chin, he did not bother to wipe it off. Carlo walked around the property and soon found a place to sit and sniff the acrid smoke. His eyes burned and yet he remained in its midst. He closed his eyes and remembered the voice of his father emanating from the beautifully dancing and inviting flames. "Bambino," it said, "take from me and share the cleansing fire with your family." Carlo responded by inserting an oak cane and lighting it. He touched the flames on the end of the cane and it felt good. Carlo stood facing each framed photograph and gleefully shared the fire with each. Glass cracked and photos scorched withering before him as he ran from room to room. He laughed happily as his father's voice screamed in his ear. "Carlo! My beautiful bambino, I am here, my son!"

Carlo stared in rapture at the remaining embers. Their bright red-hot color danced in the black and grey of the ash. He reached into the ashes and pulled out a book which smoked in his hands and blew softly into it. Carlo then walked to his neighbor's house and placed the book into a neat stack of cordwood which leaned against a back wall. The firefighters were busy and did not see him do so. The fire erupted and Carlo clapped and jumped for joy much like a child would at a pleasing sight. The fire began to consume the side of the house and Carlo cried out gleefully. "Papa! Papa! Papa! Somehow, he managed to enter the house. The occupants of the house ran out screaming towards the firefighters as the house burned behind them.

Carlo's charred corpse was discovered prostrate on a chair in the living quarters of the burned house. Oddly his face was contorted in what appeared to the mortician to be, a broad smile.

END

FLEA DEGREE

My public education experience wasn't worth a shit. No one helped me how to learn, to listen properly to understand fully. Teachers never encouraged, they literally discouraged me. "Educator," was the wrong title for most of those I knew. I don't believe they were interested in anything other than their careers. I was once called "stupid," by a teacher, a Mr. Lopez in a seventh-grade math class. The worst thing was doing it in front of the entire classroom. The pejorative stigmatized me for life. Ever since then I've never been confident doing even the most basic mathematical calculation. I trust calculators. I always wanted to learn, though.

The title of this tome refers to my experiences as a salesman in Flea Markets. As a flea-marketer you meet many types of people wanting to haggle or pay what they feel is the fairest price. I've heard so many reasons for price reductions that it's laughable. The worst are those that clearly have more than enough money in hand. Fistfuls of dollars showing and they scream for less. Appearances are very deceiving. I once lowered a price for a customer that was ragged and unkempt, he smelled of sweat and I thought "Well, this guy deserves a break." Moments later I saw him drive off in a new Mercedes. I couldn't believe my eyes, I was furious with myself! I learned though. Now I never give anyone a break. Other shop owners and I share the day talking with each other, visiting one another's shops. Most of them are smart as hell. I've learned plenty from them. I don't know if they've learned anything from me, but I take their knowledge and I apply it. That's how I know if what they offer works or not. Yeah, there's always people that come to sell on occasion, especially near the holidays but those are temps. They don't want to teach or learn a thing. They come for a quick buck and could give a shit about the customers or those of us who do this for a living. Bunch of smart asses most of them.

I had my hands on some diamonds once, the lady who brought me the jewelry, told me her mother had passed and was into costume jewelry all her life. She just wanted a single price for the lot. She didn't care to go through it to see if anything was worth something or not. She was in a hurry to go to a casino with her girlfriends and drop her quick cash. I offered her fifty-dollars and she snatched the bill out of my hand and ran off before I could say, "pleasure doing business!" As it turned out, there were several diamonds in the so called "costume," jewelry. I sold all but three (for the future, you know) for over ten thousand. The merchant I took them to, asked how I got them and almost fell out of his chair when I told him. He brought out a bottle of cognac and we drank it all. That made me wonder if I let them go for too little. I took the three I kept to another merchant and he offered two thousand a piece! I wanted to kick myself in the ass but, I did ok, I guess. Don't ask how many I sold to the first merchant it'll piss *you* off!

I met my first wife at a flea market, she didn't turn out to be a bargain in the end. Her name was Lola. *Lola! What was wrong with me?* Like, I couldn't tell a Lola was bad luck for me? Well, Lola came and went like a bargain basement item. While we were together, she took what she could, from my shop. Oh, she loved jewelry, hats - anything fancy and shiny - she wore. And I mean, she wore! All the other ladies around the market used to make fun of her while I ignored that crap. You know how people are, right? They make fun of someone who has what they want. Lola was a looker, though. She made some of that cheap stuff look like a million bucks. Damn! She had some fine hips and tits on her! She was great in bed too! Boy, those were some hot nights with Lola. But, Lola was promiscuous. She couldn't stay in one bed if it was a two bedroom town. She always found a way to make it to someone's bed. The guys around the market started talking and soon the ladies started jabbering and it slowly got to *my* ears. I wouldn't believe any of it, *no sir!* You know how people are, right? They're jealous of what others got. Well, I finally got wise and followed her home. I asked a friend to keep an eye on the shop for me. *Damned, if she wasn't doing my baby brother in my own bed! She was on her hands and knees while he was at her ass like a mangy dog*! *That son of a bitch!* And to think, I used to give him stuff for free! I threw the two out of the house and changed the damned locks. While I waited on the locksmith, I forgot to call and tell my friend watching the shop, not to give her a fucking thing. Sure enough, that rat bitch went straight to the shop and convinced him to give her the key to the register! I lost a few hundred, but it was worth getting rid of that *rat*. My little brother on the other hand, he's lucky I haven't seen him in years, otherwise I'd blow his ass to hell! *I mean it too!*

Well, I'm a loving kind a guy and guess what? I remarried a few years later. I met my second wife, yeah you guessed it, at the flea market. This time she was a vendor like me. Her shop opened next to mine quite by accident. You see, the guy who was next to me crashed his car into a semi. Died instantly! His kids, who I had known since they were in their mother's pouch, all of them; they didn't care to work his shop. I offered a good price for his wares and they sold right away. The youngest boy was the only one who cared and he cried whenever we ran into each other. Made me cry too, you know? He was the only good boy in that bunch. Damn! I'm losing my mind! I was telling you about Gloria my second wife.

Gloria sold hats, she made them, from scratch! Boy that girl could make all kinds of hats with those tiny hands of hers! Strong little hands! Gloria was small in stature but big with everything else. Smart as a whip and sharp as a tack! Yes, sir!

I approached her after she'd been in her shop a while. I wasn't in no hurry to scare her off or anything, you know? I would bring plenty of coffee in a thermos and I started visiting her and her shop, like we do around here. I wasn't interested in her at first. Once we started getting to know one another during our coffee breaks, I started to listen to her and picked up on some sage advice. She taught me to sell a bit better than I was doing. Raise my prices and such. Smile a bit more, that kind of thing. I'd forgotten to smile after Lola, as you might understand.

Gloria was not like the other lady vendors. She kept to her craft and hardly ever had the other ladies visit her shop. Usually it was men who came to say hello. She had plenty of lady customers and a couple of friends who'd stay with her some days just to keep her company, you know? It was one of her friends who made Gloria look at me differently from the other men. She told me about it months later. I never asked what exactly and it doesn't matter to me, really. I'm just glad her friend was nosy. I noticed that when I took coffee over to her, she hardly ever looked, into my eyes. She'd glance at them but never really, looked at them you know? One morning, she stared directly at them and I started shaking like a stupid kid. I couldn't look at her directly and I excused myself and left in a hurry. My shop was only a few feet away from hers, and I felt like a frightened child. I couldn't get myself to look her way, knowing I'd reveal my feelings. Somehow, and I don't know how she knew it but somehow, she knew I liked her. Listen to me! "Liked her." Like a damn kid! Hell, I fell for her right away! I loved that little thing. I'd miss her a lot on the days she didn't show up and I worked every damn day! I knew when she didn't work. Well, Gloria asked if I liked movies, and I said yes, I did. We ended up going to a movie and then another, and another until I had enough courage to take her to dinners and such. We couldn't stop seeing each other after that. I asked her to marry me and she accepted. I've never stopped loving her. Well, you know? She died a couple of years ago. Or, was it four?

She contracted cancer. Yeah contracted, like she signed a god damn paper or something. I sell her hats on occasion. I price them real high though! I like them around, they remind me of her. Yes, sir, Gloria was a good woman. She was the best! Gloria taught me at a college level, ha-ha! She sure did.

I never had kids of my own, you know? I hire kids from time to time especially when the market is busy, holidays especially. Some of these kids I've hired are so darn smart! There are some that I hire and they sit with their faces on those telephone screens, never look up! A thief could fill up his pockets with my merchandise and the kid would never know it! I take those kind by the elbow and walk them out. Some though, some are good teachers and they don't even know it! They start talking to people and I'm shocked at what they know! When we get time to sit and talk, they teach me so much! I'm happy to see these kids are going somewhere. Sometimes I think about it. Why I didn't have children of my own, you know? Wrong women when I was younger. I guess I've just been too busy selling my wares too. Gloria and I were too old. Yeah sometimes I wonder what that would 'a been like.

I've learned a lot about people through the years, being here. I see a lot of good in people, once in a while seen some bad. Most times, it's the good I see. Older folks like me are the best though. We see and feel with our hearts mostly. Yeah, I'm happy to have been here all these years and learned what I have. I'm the kind of man who can put up with most anything, but I can't stand stupid. You know? Stupid, makes me feel mad and sad. I don't know for sure, why that is? Why don't some of us learn more? If we paid more attention to each other and listened more to one another, we'd learn something! My college level flea degree means something to me. I was always open to learning, I learned plenty, learned . . . I did.

END

VISITORS

The last person who revealed state secrets concerning extraterrestrials and all things to do with the UFO enigma, was strangled with a surgical cord. Afterwards the coroner's report stated the cause of death as suicide. This individual had traveled the world for years attending conferences and making presentations revealing what he believed to be fact and, although a close friend and associate in the field had already been "disposed of," (also ruled a suicide) he pressed forth, knowing and revealing to all that would listen, that he would likely suffer the same fate. Why that man had not sought protection was puzzling to me. I had contacted him through a concerned family member, yet he chose to ignore my protection. I don't carry business cards nor do I freely advertise my services. I don't make it a point to discuss my business experience with just anyone. I only now reveal it with the hope that other whistleblowers understand, that the fear of prosecution should be the least of their worries. "They," will come for your *life*.

My name is not important; in fact it is unnecessary to reveal. I protect people. I am a former U. S. Navy Seal, International Martial Arts Champion, Peace Officer and until recently, agent for the Bureau of Indian Affairs in the OJS (Office of Justice Services). It was at the OJS that I came to understand the reason behind the suppression of Native American culture -- it has nothing to do with assimilation that is most obvious. What is not and will never be stated, is the basic truth; Native Americans can and do communicate with supernatural powers and some of those powers are extraterrestrial.

I was raised in a small rural community in the center of the Bible Belt. My parents were religious, not fanatics but devout in the sense that they practiced at home and not just church on Sunday. Yes, I was one of those boys who got whipped for misbehaving and sent to bed without supper for questioning all that my parents and teachers took for granted and I simply could not. Curiosity was and is, my worst enemy and my best friend. My father was Irish from the old country and my mother was a mixed breed of more than a handful of immigrants from several old countries. She spoke very little but got her point across when necessary and that was most of the time. My father was not a drunk per say but he could drink heavily when upset at his wife and the world, and that was quite often. Mother was the disciplinarian of the two and she could be harsh, the only time my father laid a hand to me was when I made the mistake of muttering an unkind name to my mother under my breath after one of her harshest punishments. I was twelve when I decided that rural life was not for me, so I ran from the belt straight to California.

My hitchhiking consisted of a ride from the end of my street all the way to the state of Nevada on the edge of the California border. An old Native American man picked me up thinking that I was headed to town and then he'd be done with me but, once inside his pickup I couldn't stop talking about California and it just so happened that he was going near the state. His name was Waters, he was eighty-five and a member of the tribe of Yavapai or "People of the Sun," from the state of Arizona. He spoke quietly in a near whisper and I found it hard to hear him speak with all the knocking and rattling of his old truck. He became frustrated after a few miles with my asking him to repeat himself and shot me a look of disgust and spoke no more until hours later when we came to rest off the side of a lonely road at the bottom of a starlit night. He took time to lay out a couple of blankets in the bed of the truck for me and a couple for himself in an open field. For about an hour I lay there staring at the countless stars wanting and trying *not* to think about home and my parents. They would've read my letter by now obviously, and my mother would probably be crying and my father drinking and both arguing about whose fault it was or what an ungrateful son I was. Well, I had made my decision and that was that. Yet, I still felt sorry for us all.

After that first hour, I left the truck and put down my blankets next to John. He wasn't asleep yet. He was sitting and praying or whispering to himself. I sat next to him and silently tried to make sense of him. He stopped and faced me for a few minutes and then spoke to me of the wondrous People of the Sun and their tales. Whispering mostly, he told me of the Yavapai and their language Pai. In those years, I had heard of space ships from other worlds and the possibility of aliens too but it had all been science fiction to me. As John spoke on, he talked of the Star people who had come down from the heavens on iron shields and taught the Yavapai many things and had even given them their true name. He wasn't just saying these things to make conversation I could tell he believed everything he was imparting with all his heart and soul and he wanted me to believe it too. With tears in his eyes, he talked about the decimation of his people and the cruel white man who had lied over and over every time they spoke. My heart felt heavy and it was with the strongest sense of despair and guilt that I apologized for all the wrongs committed by our people on his and all native peoples of this world. He nodded but I knew my apology would never be healing enough no matter how sincere. In the distant and dark horizon, we saw what appeared to be a bright star and after a minute or two, it moved ever so slightly and then rapidly shot straight up to the heavens. John simply smiled and continued nodding at me. I could not imagine what it was that we had seen, it was just one of those odd things that happen without needing explaining. I shrugged my shoulders and lay back on the blankets not knowing or caring what time of the night it was.

I had no idea how long I had been asleep when John shook me awake. He had startled me and I quickly jumped up wide eyed and fearful! I suddenly realized where I was and who he was but I could hardly see him in the pitch dark.

John knew I couldn't see very well so, he took my arm and raised it in the darkness to the sky directly above us, I almost fell to the ground in shock. A reddish spherical light glowed in the dark sky and it appeared to grow as I stood there on shaky legs. It kept dropping at a slow pace and it grew as it came down toward us. I grew scared and would have run off if John hadn't held me in place with a powerful grip. Tears started to run down my cheeks as I shook, I began wetting myself but could not move.

The object touched ground a few yards from where we stood but it was no longer a reddish color, it threw off a light golden hue. There was no sound, not even the crickets which had kept us company through the night were chirping, I was frightened yet John made me feel a bit calmer. He began to whisper his prayers and started walking towards the object with me in tow. I could hardly move my legs but John held me firm and pulled me along. He turned to me and in the golden glow I could see his face clearly. He smiled and raised his arms to the sky, palms out. For a moment, I thought he'd fall to his knees in worship but he simply stood there murmuring his incantations. Shaking like a wet puppy I could only stare at this, this thing.

My legs stopped shaking and I was beginning to calm further the longer I stood there with nothing else happening. I then focused my attention on the details of what I began to finally think of as a space ship, or saucer. I was amazed to see that it was almost translucent. *Was that movement I saw?* I felt like I was being watched from inside. Somehow, I received a message of some sort that everything was going to be alright. I couldn't understand how or why but I knew that it or someone inside was communicating with me and John. I felt warm in what was a cold evening, my breath could be seen when I opened my mouth even though I could not speak. I asked many questions and received many replies even though some of my questions were not answered, I felt as though I already somehow knew the answers. I smiled and laughed at one point. I had never felt so alive! I reached over and hugged John as he continued to smile and talk to these beings. I squinted trying to make out the figures in the bright light and at one point I thought I saw one stand up and wave at me. It was as though they were in some type of cocoon or membrane that was transparent yet, opaque at the same time.

I felt frustrated, wanting and needing to see who and what these beings were. I felt like a child (which I truly was) in a store seeing toys, wanting them but knowing I'd be unable to own or hold them.

Why did I want to see them anyway? Wasn't it enough knowing they were present and talking to me?

For a fraction of a second it was as though they understood my frustration and cleared my view and I finally saw them.

I don't remember when I fell asleep or how I got back onto the bed of that old truck, I simply opened my eyes to a beautiful dawn and saw John bundled up in his blankets smiling and snoring away. Did I dream last night's event? I was confused yet I felt happy, happier than I had ever felt before. I stood up and walked over to the side of the truck and urinated through a rust hole. I looked out into the field and spotted what looked like a dark patch of scorched grass. I zipped up and as I drew closer to the circular spot, I could smell something I'd never smelled before. Now years later, I can categorically state that the scent was that of ozone. The grass was scorched in a circular pattern and I could see where footprints were made in the dirt near and around the area and they all came and went from where we had slept and to the truck. No, it hadn't been a dream.

John awoke and began to collect the blankets, he turned around and relieved himself he apparently wasn't as modest, as I.

Two days later we parted company. I waved as John drove off, he never looked back.

My life was forever changed by that experience. I know that one day when I least expect it, those people will return and give me a bit more knowledge than they had that fateful evening. One thing I can confirm and know in my heart, they are not extraterrestrial; they are us.

END

MORE

Carl methodically swept the floor of his wife's beauty salon taking care not to leave a hair or a speck of debris anywhere. Helen his wife, laughed out loud while teasing a client's hair, a light blue. This particular customer had been one of the first to visit the shop when she first opened for business in 2014. Now, thirty years later her once light auburn hair was died a light blue to match her age and that of her dearest friends. Helen paid close attention to details heard from her clients of other clients and knew just about all there was to know of them all. She wasn't the type to hold back in disseminating all that juicy gossip, she'd be the first to tell anyone sitting in her chair all the lurid and exciting tales shared in her trade. But this story is about Carl.

Carl Buell met Helen in of all places, a beauty salon. He'd known the owner, Dave and his male partner, Darrell since their university days. Dave and Darrell were partners in and out of the business. While Carl waited his turn at Darrell's chair, Helen walked in and he completely fell for her. He sat quietly as she sat next to him reading an old glamour magazine. Carl finally built up enough courage to talk to her. They chatted for a while until it was Carl's turn for a haircut. Before leaving his chair, Helen asked if he would like her number and Carl nearly fell backwards hurrying back to take it. He called her that afternoon and set a dinner date. A year later they married. Dave and

Darrell's beauty salon came up for sale five years later when Dave fell ill and suddenly died one evening in their home, wrapped in Darrell's strong and loving arms. Darrell could not face returning to the business, so he sold the salon to Carl and moved to San Francisco. Helen had always wished for her own business and when Carl offered to buy it as a fifth anniversary present she was stunned.

Carl had been interested in science and science fiction from childhood. He had collected books and magazines that literally filled the entire house. He especially became interested in the idea of cloning and its possibilities. Through the years, he'd communicated with scientists in the field for decades and was acquainted with many on a first name basis. Some had taken time to visit Carl at his home and he proudly displayed photos of himself with many of these luminaries. He was so voiced in the parlance of the specific science that some thought he should continue his studies and join in their research. Flattered by their sentiments, Carl would nod happily but never took them up on it.

Carl's parents had died in an automobile accident while he was still in high school and having been wealthy, left him with a substantial fortune which he used quite judiciously. He was extremely careful with his money and hadn't told Helen how much he was actually worth. As far as Helen knew, Carl's parents had left him enough to live a decent life in an average home with an average lifestyle. Carl was worth well over eighty million dollars, he had made a vow after his parent's death never to brag or show off his wealth. He had seen what money had done to his parents and their so called friends and did not want to experience it himself. He had wanted to earn good and decent friends on his own merits and not attract false ones through wealth as his parents had.

Helen had come into his life years later. Carl had dated only a handful of women and most eventually grew tired of his frugal ways. They all complained of his lack of ambition or drive for increase, having only enough money to get by with and they wanted more for themselves through him. He had not met one whom he could trust due to their demanding "needs." Even now he was debating whether he should go ahead and reveal his truth to Helen even after having been married this long, even though she had not once complained of wanting more. Yet, something kept holding him back. He was beginning to believe that he had truly missed out on women. The more he contemplated the idea, the more he came to believe it was the cause of his reluctance to reveal his worth to Helen. Slowly Carl began to recede into himself.

For ten years Carl kept Helen's beauty salon in order. He especially loved sweeping the floors. He did the accounting and answered the phone setting appointments for her clients, buying and stocking supplies and doing anything Helen requested. After all these years of having Carl around the salon, Helen had almost forgotten about him as a husband, she had begun several years ago to treat him as a servant. Carl would only nod as she berated him in front of her clients, some of which felt sorry for him and others who simply shook their heads silently in his presence and laughed along with Helen in his absence.

Carl was methodical. When a client he found rather beautiful or attractive would have her hair done, he quickly headed to the just vacated chair and would collect their hair, carefully sealing samples in plastic vials. Through the years he collected dozens of samples which he carefully labeled by name and date. He had journals in which he wrote down their natural and false color application dates, age and specific look being careful to also list any changes in behavior. Of all the women he'd saved samples of, only four stood out as best candidates. He separated the four special vials and began his experiments.

Eleven years after marriage, Carl had bought himself a small laboratory only three miles from the salon. He'd filled the lab with all the equipment and supplies needed for his undertaking. He had advertised for a select group of scientists and under an assumed name hired those he believed would be able to fulfill his goal of cloning a fully functioning human specimen.

The laboratory experiments were costly to say the least. The scientists proved to be hardheaded and independent. Carl did his best to keep them on point and working as a team. He was given no choice but to release two who had been most difficult to work with the others. Feeling less pressured the remainder were more cohesive and the work moved forward efficiently and at substantially reduced cost. Carl's vision was closely becoming reality.

Helen's verbal attacks began to weigh heavily on Carl. He'd ignored the majority of her bitching through the years but Helen had grown more abusive. Recently she noticed Carl was not cleaning the salon as well as he had in the past and was taking too long in returning from whatever errands he ran. Once, he forgot to empty the trash cans and she threw one at him in anger as her last appointment left the shop. Carl took the brunt of the force on his right forearm blocking the can which cut him deeply causing it to bleed profusely. Instead of apologizing for her behavior, Helen screamed that it was his fault. She demanded that he clean up her mess and angrily stormed out. Carl sat on the empty salon chair and smiled a slightly twisted grin at his reflection in the large mirror as the blood from his forearm soaked the hairy floor.

At home early for the first time in months, Carl methodically packed a pair of suitcases with a few of Helen's clothes. He walked into the bathroom and loaded a plastic sack with Helen's personal items. Next, he boxed more of her belongings and carried them to the front door. He looked around for photographs he knew she'd want and while doing so, the locksmith changed locks on all entryways including replacing the garage door opener. Satisfied that he was doing the right thing, Carl loaded all and drove to Helen's beauty salon. He entered through the back door and could hear Helen and her latest client laughing loudly while sharing who knew what gossip. He made little noise as he unloaded her possessions and finally entered the salon to Helen's surprise. Carl called to her but she ignored him and continued gossiping with her client who kept touching her new hairdo. Carl slowly approached Helen, handed her a folded note and walked away towards the back of the shop as she slowly unfolded the paper. He heard her scream as he closed and locked the rear door.

Months later at the laboratory, Carl met with his team who excitedly revealed their breakthrough. They had finally and successfully cloned a complete human being with a catch. The subject had been a young girl who it later turned up had shown signs of cerebral palsy, which had gone undetected for some unknown reason and was presently wheelchair bound. The clone which was a fully developed adult, had also developed the cerebral palsy but at an accelerated rate and was now bent and crippled. They asked Carl for permission to "dispose,' of the "body."

Further work continued after the last debacle. The scientists and doctors managed to produce four fully adult female clones from the collected hair samples. All females were alert but functioning at early childhood levels. Months of therapy, education and support were provided for their survival and wellbeing. Carl explained to the team that these women would be well cared for out of country where they would not be subjected to scrutiny. The team while not wanting to release the subjects to anyone's custody without their consent was then led to further experimentation, but now on male subjects.

Slowly, Carl began to release the scientists surreptitiously one by one. He methodically fired the team and then abandoned the laboratory. To assure total silence he hired a mercenary to eliminate all former employees. According to Carl the cost of silence was more than well worth it. As an afterthought, he asked that his ex-wife Helen be taken care of just for fun. After the eliminations, he invited the killer to join him at his recently purchased home in the Cayman Islands to enjoy a month of recreation with a group of young compliant ladies. As the mercenary flew to the islands in Carl's private jet it mysteriously exploded in midair crashing into the sea.

Carl was finally satisfied. He lacked nothing and was now totally free of connections to his past. The four beautiful females which he now owned and controlled in his luxurious mansion by the sea were his and his alone.

END

WOLF

The creature smelled of the wild and dense forest; it had never known a companion. His life had been of solitude, but one he would soon change.

The scent of humans, another predatory creature who seemed to appear and disappear more often now than ever before, was increasing, encroaching in his territory. Baring its fangs in disgust, the wolf sniffed the air and sure enough, he smelled them near.

The humans were too busy setting camp to feel the wolf's presence. They laughed and spoke loudly making themselves known for a great distance. The female of the pair decided to hunt for small dry branches and grasses, so as to start a campfire. She felt comfortable and at ease in the forest and having her companion nearby added to her sense of security. The male continued to clear the area of brush and formed a stone ring for the upcoming blaze.

The wolf could clearly see the pair from his hilltop vantage point. He sniffed and licked the air several times in disgust at the intruders but dared not approach as he had seen how deadly they could be. The air did not taste of gun smoke nor had he heard the thunderous sound of gunfire thus giving *him* a sense of security. He growled deeply and laid down resting his head on his forepaws, staring at the couple for hours.

The humans sang and laughed, enjoying the setting sun while the wolf slept peacefully dreaming of his coming meal.

The campfire was slowly dying away. The humans did not feed the pit further as the stars and a partial moon lit the forest and camp. Wolf had neared the tent and its sleeping occupants stealthily, not a sound was made by his approach. He could smell humanity and all its articles. No sounds were heard from the tent as wolf lay on the ground, waiting. After a lifetime of hunting, wolf had learned human behavior. One human or both would wake and exit the tent to relieve themselves. They were all the same. Humans who came out often eventually found themselves comfortable enough to forget protection from animals of the forest. Forgetting weapons or lights, they often fearlessly or forgetfully walked away from their tents not expecting danger. Sometimes, a smart one would feed a few sticks to the fire or come prepared but not too often. Wolf sat staring at the tent sensing the human's behavior. It was not long before one human began to stir, wolf felt his heartbeat rise and stir as well.

The female unzipped and exited the tent, she held something in her hand but wolf could see it was neither a weapon nor a light. She fell to the ground on both hands and knees, she cursed and stood erect wiping her knees and hands. She quietly laughed at her clumsiness. Looking up at the sky her face was clear to wolf. He sniffed the air and watched as she walked away from the camp. Squatting against a tree she urinated and wolf's excitement rose and he quickly stood on all fours. Slowly he crept between the trees sniffing the air and looking towards the tent making sure the other human was still.

The woman fully stood raising her pants while looking up at the stars and moon. Taking a deep breath, she stretched her lithe body and then bent at the waist to touch her toes. Wolf was near her, she never felt nor heard him. She twisted her body at the waist and put her arms out to her sides while flexing her hands. The woman's left hand brushed against wolf's right ear and she reflexively pulled away. Wolf sensed her fear and felt her heartbeat rise. The woman stood perfectly still, tears began to fall from her eyes as her throat tightened into a knot. Her body shook uncontrollably and from deep inside she began to urinate once more. Wolf smelled the urine and opened his mouth, tongue pulled back, teeth bared ready to snap. For a fraction of a second both froze in place.

Not sure why, woman slowly reached out touching wolf's head. Wolf closed his mouth, lowered his shoulders and then sat on his hind legs. Wolf had felt something in the woman's touch. Confusion ran through his mind, something he had *never* experienced. He suddenly felt calm and rubbed his head against her hand. A thought suddenly gripped wolf. He pictured the den of his youth. His Mother's snuggles and warm teat came to mind, he remembered her *love*.

Woman pressed her leg against wolf's chest and rubbed wolf's head more vigorously. She placed her right hand against his lower jaw and squeezed affectionately. She had never touched a wolf before but was quite familiar with canines, as she had grown up surrounded by them. Her heart warmed and all the fear washed away. Wolf smiled and pressed himself tighter against the woman's leg. He whimpered as her hands moved away but calmed as they returned and now hugged his huge chest. Woman bent down and placed her face against the side of wolf's shoulder. She felt and heard his heartbeat. His warm chest rose and fell against her hot moist cheek. She smelled wolf, filling her lungs with his strong scent. They both lay on the ground together and snuggled.

Wolf closed his eyes and felt like a pup once again. He could not understand how a human could make him feel so, *good*. Was it possible to feel a human's love?

Woman felt in her heart that this massive wolf would not harm her. She could not fully understand how that was but she accepted it completely. Her years as an empath had turned magical. Her childhood had been rough, with parents that were less than caring or loving. Somehow, she had become the adult in the small family, taking care of her parent's needs. All her young life had been spent in making sure her parents made it through each day without causing themselves or her, pain. Always needy, her parents both accepted and rejected their child. Woman had one day noticed that when she touched someone or something she felt what they felt. It wasn't strong at first but slowly she began to accept her gift and began building on it. She once collected several dogs from the streets and each had a different need that she instinctively knew. Those dogs loved her immensely and she them. For several years, she cared for this large family, both human and animal. Her parents did not like that the dogs were given more attention and at one point decided to get rid of them while girl was at school. Upon her return, girl couldn't understand why her parents had done this horrible thing and in a fit of rage, promised that she would never help her parents again. The parents also grew angry and told girl to leave their house. Girl left them and never returned.

Years later, girl became a woman and cared for many animals with a man who cared for her and animals too. Her empathic abilities had matured and grown.

Wolf received those images from woman's touch, heart, and mind and it all felt *good*. Woman fed him cooked meat from the fire pit and water from bottles that tasted different to wolf. He had never thought of humans as kind. All his life he had been hunted and had seen many of his kind killed and taken away. Now he felt confused but understood that this woman loved him.

The human man had at first watched woman and wolf from a distance. He shook his head and marveled at the sight. His heart felt love for wolf also and it wasn't long before wolf, feeling it, slowly approached man with head bowed. When man first touched him, wolf did not feel anything. He thought he would feel something like the woman's touch, but he did not. The man's hands rubbed his chest, legs and head and it wasn't long before wolf felt he could trust this human man.

Hours later, all three were playing in a meadow frolicking like children. Chasing one another and tumbling against each other. Wolf felt good. Both woman and man felt good.

With sun blazing above them, they played like children. Woman and man teased wolf with a stick. Wolf behaved like a happy playful pup, running and fetching the huge stick until there was nothing left of it. Wolf was running towards the couple when he suddenly fell flat on his face. The roar of the rifle's sound followed in a millisecond. As he lay bleeding to death, wolf felt good. He had experienced love once more and smiled as his lungs emptied and eyes slowly shut. Wolf would never know that a human had murdered him.

Woman's lungs burst into a high-pitched scream. Man, stopped in his tracks also screaming at the top of his lungs. Both looked towards the direction of the rifle's sound and saw two men running towards them. Both hunters looked frightened and concerned for the couple. Reaching them, they were attacked with punches and kicks. They would never understand why.

END

WITHOUT MARIA

She told me she'd been born in Mexico City. She lied. Her parents had abandoned her as a child, she'd sadly whispered. Another lie. She introduced herself as Maria Lourdes Escobar. Her name, I was told by the police, was Luna de la Paz. She'd been born in the barrios of Guatemala to a fifteen-year-old Indian girl. She was gone now. Vanished like the multitude of lies and stories she'd created.

We first met at a fundraiser for a non-profit charity back in two thousand and three. Maria, or rather Luna, was beautiful. She flitted about the small group of people like a butterfly on a sugar high. Her smile was breathtaking and her amber eyes contrasted vividly with her bronzed skin. At first I thought she was just another tanned party-minded trust fund baby, but I was wrong, dead wrong.

I dismissed her lighthearted flirty talk as just a way to help the charity raise money. She asked if I spent money on "trinkets," for my "girls?" as she put it, laughing as she asked.

My answer was a simple but emphatic, "No."

"Are you saving all your money for the future?" she inquired.

"I'm saving it to buy a boat," I answered with a smile.

"Yacht?" or "fishing?"

"Neither one, I'm saving for a catamaran." "I plan on sailing the Pacific coast for a year or two."

"Wow!" That sounds like fun!" "Need a first-mate?" "Or, have you taken care of that already?" she teased.

"First-mate?" Actually I hadn't thought of taking anyone along, but the thought of *you*, is enticing."

She smiled, took my elbow in her hand and led me to the bar.

We talked about ourselves and life in general, idle chatter mostly. I was impressed with her poise and beauty. I noticed several people staring at us, feeling uncomfortable I asked her outdoors, without hesitation I led her. The night air was fresh and cool; it was such a relief from the air-conditioned perfumed stuffiness.

Without much thought, I pulled her close and placed my face next to her cheek. Her skin was soft and warm, with the slightest scent of peach, making my mouth water. She didn't pull back, matching my boldness.

"Like what you see?" she asked.

"I do."

"Is that all you wish, the sight of me?"

"I wish for all you're willing to surrender."

"Wow, you're not at all shy, are you?" she smiled hugely.

"If I hesitate, it perhaps may be too late."

"Well, I wonder, are you *ever* late?"

"Not intentionally."

"Sometimes it's worth waiting."

"It depends."

"On what perhaps?"

"Whether you gamble or not."

"Gamble?"

"Are you willing to chance losing a moment or an opportunity by hesitating?"

"I see."

"Do you?"

"I don't gamble."

"We gamble with our lives every day. Do I make a turn here? Do I rebuff him or not?" "Every moment is at stake."

"I don't think in those terms, really." "Life is a gamble I suppose, but I never think of every moment as an opportunity to win or lose something."

"I do. And right now, I'm betting that you'll leave with me and not be overcome with remorse in the morning."

"You lose." And with that she was off.

I saw her at an art exhibit two months later. She smiled broadly and rushed to greet me.

"I thought I'd never see you again!"

"I thought we might see one another once more. Although, I thought it might have been sooner."

"I pictured you sailing around Hawaii with your first-mate."

"Not yet, it won't be long though."

"Is the position still open then?"

"Why yes, it is."

"Well what are you waiting for? Aren't you going to ask?"

"Maria, will you be my first-mate?"

"I can't."

"You are such a tease." I turned away feeling foolish for falling into that silly trap.

"Wait!" "What I meant is that, I can't right now, but I will in two months."

"This is my number, call me when you're prepared to sail."

"By the way, who are you? "What is your name?

"Octavio Ari Narvaez."

"Octavio, I like that, it sounds *powerful, sensual*."

"Very nice. I look forward to your call."

I walked away reinvigorated.

The next six weeks were spent in preparation. I felt an urgency to complete my task and a yearning to see Maria and have her in my arms. I stocked provisions enough to carry us through a couple of weeks. We truly didn't need much but I'd rather be prepared for any eventuality. I'll gamble for money and items of interest, but I refuse to gamble with my life or that of another in my charge. I hoped Maria would be physically capable and willing to assist in handling my boat. Surprisingly the catamaran had not taken a large portion of my savings. I'd found an old salt who'd reluctantly become a land lubber. He gave me such an unbelievable deal. I could not refuse. He bought himself an RV and set sail for America's open roads. The boat was surprisingly clean and larger than I'd wanted, but it was too good to pass up. I'd been on others that were too confining, especially in the height department. This one accommodated taller people which made me feel quite comfortable.

At the end of the eight week stretch, Maria called.

"Hello, Captain?"

"Aye!"

"Are you ready for boarding?"

"One crewmate, yes."

"Given proper directions, I'll be at the dock with satchel in tow first thing in the morning."

"Aye, aye."

She stood at the dock smiling and deeply tanned as though boarding from one ship to another. I stood on board and stared. She let her satchel drop, stood at ramrod attention and saluted sharply.

I laughed welcoming her on board.

"You amaze me, Maria."

"Yes?"

"Yes, you look spectacular. Your tan is magnificent!"

"Several sessions at the salon can do wonders."

"Salon? You purchased a tan?"

"Of course, you didn't think I was in the sun all this time, did you?"

"Why, yes. I thought you might have sunned at your poolside"

"This is a *full* body salon tan, sir!"

My knees went weak hearing that. I turned away not wanting her to know how I felt.

"M*y* quarters, Captain?"

"Follow me, mate."

Maria inspected the catamaran staring and touching everything. She asked question after question, some I couldn't answer.

"How many boats have you sailed, Octavio?"

Hearing her say my name brought a smile to my lips. I couldn't stop smiling.

"One."

"One?"

"Yes, one. It was a typical sailboat not a catamaran."

"And when was that?"

"I was a teenager, it belonged to a friend."

"Teenager?" "Did you actually sail it, or were you a guest?"

"Yes, I sailed it." "My friend was afraid of water, she let me sail."

"She?" interesting."

"Strictly *plutonic*, we were very young, great friends."

"Did you ever fantasize sexually over her?"

"No, like I said, we were kids."

"Did her parents not approve?"

"Her parents were...wealthy."

"The answer is yes, then?"

"*Yes*, they did not approve of me."

"So, what eventually happened to your *friend*?"

"She drowned."

"Did you say, drowned?"

"An accident."

"Were you the cause of that unfortunate accident?"

"What?" "No!" "No, her father grew angry at her for sneaking about with me." "He refused to take her fear seriously. One day he caught us and made me stay on shore while he sent her out on the lake. He forced her onto a sloop. She could swim in a pool but the vastness of the lake frightened her. He pushed her off, she cried and shook, but he was too angry to hear her pleas. He screamed at her as a gust

blew her farther away, she sobbed hysterically. He held me back, and told me never to come back. He threatened to beat me and send me to jail if I did. As I turned away I glanced back and saw that the sloop had capsized. Pulling from his grip I ran, diving off the dock I swam as fast as I could. My arms grew weak; I couldn't reach her. A lifeboat brought her body ashore. She looked, calm."

"I shouldn't have asked."

"That's alright, it's been years."

"Forgive me."

"It's fine. I hadn't thought of Mary in years."

"Mary?"

"Yes, her name was Mary."

"That is interesting."

"Coincidence..."

"Ok. Well; O? What would you like me to do?"

"O?"

"Yeah, *O*."

"Now, that is interesting. I thought Octavio was powerful?"

"It is, but *O* is easy on the lips."

"How about *Captain* O, mate?"

"Aye, aye, *Captain O* it is!"

"Alrighty mate, time to set sail!"

We sailed down the Baja Peninsula for some fishing and coastal touring. The waters were choppy, the main sail full, the lesser sails full and the flag flapping loudly in the sun. I was truly relaxed for the first time in months, hell, *years!* Maria and I hadn't yet found the intimacy I had anticipated and fantasized on. In the evening, we talked, ate, drank then fall asleep where we sat. During the day, we'd lounge around not speaking, simply enjoying the sights and sounds of the sea and the coast. On the fourth day, I was repairing one of the deadeye supports to a sail's lanyard when Maria walked out on deck wearing nothing. I couldn't take my eyes off her. She had gotten darker but now I could see tan lines where she had said there were none. She looked out to sea and never glanced my way. I couldn't help myself. I walked up to her and wrapped my arms around her, she smelled of sun and salt. She kissed my forearms and rested her head against my wrist. At that moment, I felt whole.

Docked, I called out to Maria. She came up with a plate of fruit and glasses of wine. I hadn't expected to kick back at that moment. I'd planned on going ashore to locate a place for dining. Maria pressed herself against my side and asked me to sit and enjoy a few minutes on deck. I told her we needed provisions and planned on making a few purchases that afternoon. She chose to stay onboard and clean up before taking a nap under the main sail. I left her below deck after we'd spent time making love.

Hours later as I walked towards the dock, I saw that my cat was gone. I looked around thinking that maybe Maria had been forced to move her. Of course, that never would have been the case, but I was hopeful. No, she was gone.

The county Sherriff and a Deputy shook their heads looking forlorn. A call had been put out to the Coast Guard and they would hopefully locate my cat. The Sherriff placed his beefy hand on my shoulder and asked how long I'd known Maria. I sheepishly admitted a short while. He shook his head, looked down and spit on the ground next to my sandaled foot. The Deputy then spat on top of the Sherriff's spittle. He laughed at having hit the mark and gently nudged the Sherriff's shoulder. They both turned and walked away. Entering the patrol car, the Sherriff asked if I might need a ride to a hotel. I shook my head and waved them off, not wanting their company.

The motel room was clean and comfortable. I paid the clerk, who eyed me and the grocery bags suspiciously. He didn't ask, simply handing me the key before turning back to an old black and white television set. I placed what I could in the small refrigerator and lay down on the bed. I wondered why Maria had disappeared with my boat. I began to wonder if maybe she'd been kidnapped. Maybe someone saw me leave the cat and knew Maria was alone onboard. Maybe this, maybe that. I fell asleep and was awakened by a knock on the door. The Sherriff was back without his Deputy.

"Sir, the Coast Guard reported no luck spotting your boat. They're wondering if maybe you made up a story for some odd reason. You see, the Guard doesn't usually fail to locate a boat such as yours or any boat for that matter! They can cover a huge area in no time. But, well, they couldn't locate yours.

I didn't know what to think anymore, I sat on the corner of the bed. I finally convinced the Sherriff that I had not made up the story. He stared at me then spat on the ground, wiped his mouth and nodded.

"We'll see then." and walked away.

Just before entering his car, he looked up, "Don't leave the motel or town!"

I thought it extremely odd that the Coast Guard hadn't located my cat. Did Maria have boating experience? Had she acted like a novice only to highjack my boat? What would she do with her? Where would she go? I fell asleep.

Maria was smiling down at me. I quickly sat up and realized I'd been dreaming. I grew angry and grabbed a beer out of the fridge. I cracked it open and chugged it all down. My face was hot and my heart beat like a native drum. I grew angrier the more I thought about her. Why would she do it, I wondered? Had she done this before and to whom? Was she a thief? What else was she? Who the hell, was she? I felt like the proverbial village idiot. "Your mind was on fucking her, you damned idiot!" I shouted to myself. I could do nothing but wait. I chose to find a restaurant with a bar just to get out of the confining room and get some grub and a hard drink or two.

The waitress smiled and stood by waiting for my order. I asked if she'd mind coming back while I decided. She walked away and took her time coming back. I placed my order and waited for my drink. The waitress returned and asked if everything was alright. I nodded and she walked away once more. I drank three Scotch and waters and began to feel a bit calmer. After the steak and potatoes, I ordered another Scotch, neat. After paying my tab, I walked to the bar and ordered another Scotch. The bartender was generous and smiled knowingly. She started the conversation by asking if I was the guy whose boat had gotten stolen. I looked around the bar and laughed.

"Does the Sherriff come in for drinks?" I asked her.

"He's my husband."

"Oh?"

"He described you and when I saw you enter, I knew it was you he told me about."

"I see," was all I could think to say.

"Not much interesting happens here."

"I thought not."

"What do you plan on doing? I mean if you don't get your boat back?"

"I suppose I'll have to get myself home, somehow."

"Staying at the motel?"

"Yes, the one you can see from the front window there. Didn't you see me come from there?"

"Sorry. Yes, I did."

"I needed to get out, I was only growing angrier and angrier unable to do anything."

"I understand."

"Do you, now?"

"Well, I mean you getting angrier and feeling helpless and all."

"Sure, of course. I'm sorry, I didn't mean to sound like such an asshole."

"That's alright, I talk to assholes all the time. I know when they mean it and not."

"Thanks."

"Hey! Why don't you go back to the hotel before the Sherriff picks you up for being out in public while intoxicated?"

"Is it that obvious?"

"Well, I am a professional. I know a drunk when I see one." she laughed.

I rose from the stool and left her a nice tip. I waved "bye" and stumbled off.

I closed the door behind me and fell on the tiny bed. I don't know how long I had been laying there when I was startled by a hand on my shoulder. I looked back and saw the bartender next to the bed. She'd removed her clothes and began pulling at my shorts. I almost kicked her away before I decided to just let her do as she was. She grabbed my dick and put it in her mouth. I closed my eyes as she squeezed my chest and arms. She was ravenous! Her eyes were closed and she looked to be in a trance. Her hair was overflowing and felt soft in my hands. I grabbed her head and pushed my cock further into her. I came and she looked up at me and smiled. Her breasts were pressed against my legs and I watched as she slowly pulled herself up and fell against my chest.

"Mmmmmm, that was delicious," she purred.

I didn't respond. I slowly ran a hand over her back and shoulder feeling her soft hot skin. I didn't want to think about her husband but he came to mind and I felt a touch of panic.

"Where's your husband?" I asked.

"Oh, he's probably fucking one of his girlfriends."

"Ok. I see now why you came over."

"You looked in need of comforting."

"And you needed some..."

"Yes, I needed a fuck."

"Well, now that that's cleared up, I don't need to be frightened of the Sherriff?"

"No. He usually spends the evenings with one or another friend."

"Friend? That's interesting."

"It is."

"And where will you go from here?"

"Home, of course."

"That's good. You could stay the night if you wish."

"Love too but that skinny freak will probably tell my husband I was here, if he sees me in the morning."

"Doesn't he sleep?"

"He's asleep now, that's why I came in. You didn't lock the door you know."

"Didn't think about it. I guess I was too tired."

"I'm glad you didn't."

"Me too."

The clerk stared at me as I handed him the key and for a moment I thought the bastard knew about the Sherriff's wife. No, if he'd known, I'd probably be dead or in handcuffs right now. I nodded and walked to the cab. The cab driver smiled and asked if I had any luggage. The hotel room was spacious and luxurious. I'd been here for a week and had bought clothes and rested. I hadn't heard from anyone concerning my cat and had come to conclude, that I never would. The loss had hurt but I'd always made contingency plans in my life and would recover once the insurance company paid. I had a hell of a time explaining to them but eventually I was believed or at least they didn't want to hear any more and would be sending a check promptly.

In the meantime, the search was on for Luna De La Paz aka; Maria Lourdes Escobar.

As I slowly walked in to the grand lobby of The Marquis, I scanned the area for Maria. I was told she'd be here. The private detective had shown me photos of her and her "husband." She had attached herself to whom I was told, was a professional thief. It didn't surprise me that she had hooked up with an accomplice. I was told that this is common among thieves.

I saw her walking arm in arm with an older gentleman who appeared to be two or three decades her senior. Both stylishly dressed and quite the couple. I followed them discreetly and watched as they played their roles. I saw how Maria would reach out and squeeze a man's arm and press her hip against a leg or buttock. Teasing, always teasing and testing. They were smooth operators. He would place an arm around the waist of a woman, usually older than he and pull her tightly to him. I watched as he'd run his hand over a bare back and on occasion lightly pinch a buttock. The ladies, of course loved the attention and the men Maria worked responded in kind. She was the bolder of the two. I watched as she reached and grabbed a man's front at a discreet angle, causing the man to flinch and quickly recover with a smile. One older gentleman was so startled that he squealed like a girl. Maria laughed loudly and grabbed his elbow pulling him to her to hide the obvious. The gent finally pulled away from her and quickly rushed to the gentlemen's room. He'd probably urinated in his pants. Maria simply laughed and casually made her way to the next target.

I finally had seen enough. The private detective who had been in attendance had photographed quite a bit and left. We'd meet tomorrow.

I stood at the bar knowing Maria was slowly approaching from behind. With my back to her and my head bowed, I waited until she tapped me on the shoulder and waited for me to turn to her. As she waited she lightly spoke to the other men who were excited to have her near. Her hand did not leave my shoulder until I turned and faced her. She quickly pulled away as though touched by a flame! Regaining her composure, she smiled grandly.

"Oh Oscar, it's so good to see you!"

"Octavio," I corrected her with a smile.

"Why of course, how rude of me to forget! So how are you Octavio?"

I simply smiled and stared at her.

She appeared a little ruffled but kept up the charade.

"So, did you ever travel the world as you had planned?"

I was a bit surprised at her gall. I slowly shook my head.

"I managed to go out to sea for a few days when I ran into a horrible storm."

"Horrible?"

"Yes, it was devastating, I lost her at sea."

"And you're here, you survived."

"Yes, I survived to tell about it."

"To tell what exactly?"

"Well, I have much to tell."

"Perhaps another time when we're not so busy socializing with other guests?"

"Of course, another time perhaps."

She slowly made her way to her husband and gently led him to the main doors while whispering in his ear. The gentleman did not look back but was instead smiling and nodding to guests as they exited.

I didn't follow, I'd hired someone for that.

Maria was alone in her suite when I knocked. She opened the door and was shocked to see me. She attempted to close it; my shoe however, blocked the way. She opened it fully making a grand gesture allowing me to enter.

The apartment was quite extravagant, well appointed. She sat on a loveseat spreading her bathrobe over a leg partially exposing her nakedness. I walked the room looking and touching everything. She smiled when she remembered she'd done the same on my catamaran.

"And what do you plan on confiscating?"

"Confiscate? Is that what you did, Luna? Confiscate?"

"Luna? You confuse me with someone else, my name is Maria."

"No, your name is Luna."

"How interesting, you know so much and here I am knowing so little."

"You know enough."

"Do I?"

"Si."

"What are your intentions?"

"You'll soon know."

"How soon?"

"When you next hear a knock on your door."

"And who would be knocking?"

"Destiny, karma."

"And what will my destiny be, Octavio?"

"That is up to a judge."

"There is no judge that will be a part of my destiny."

"No? We'll see."

"You don't understand my friend. I own many judges."

"Friend? So, you steal from your friends?"

"Sarcasm, when I call you friend."

"Understood."

"As I said, there is no judge that will have me in their court. You are out of luck."

"The judge I have in mind is not in this town. Not of this country. To be precise."

"So, now you are into kidnapping? My, my, you are now, a criminal?

"I suppose I am."

"What do you want, Octavio?"

"Octavio, now. How interesting. I must be touching a sensitive nerve."

"What do you want? Money? Your boat?"

"Justice."

"Justice? That is hilarious!"

"At this moment, it may be to you. To me, well, it is simple. Simple justice."

"And where do you propose to take me?"

"That is of no consequence to you. Your *"husband,"* is already on his way."

"Is he?"

"Yes. He'll arrive tonight. You my dear, will arrive tomorrow morning."

"Octavio, may we negotiate?"

"Negotiate? No, no negotiating."

"Where will my husband be tonight?"

"Mejico."

"Mejico, Octavio? Please, can we make a deal?

"No deals for you, *Luna*. This is your destiny. Remember?"

"Everyone negotiates. *Especially in Mexico!"*

"That does happen on occasion, I must admit. Dear, Luna. I have never negotiated. You see my dear Luna, as a retired military general, I have my own rules. I have always had my own rules."

"Octavio, please, please! I beg you! Do not take me to your home!"

"Luna, please show me to your safe?"

"My safe?"

"Yes, safe."

"Of course! My safe! Yes, Yes! I have plenty of money and jewelry. All the jewelry is genuine, no fake gems and diamonds. Platinum and gold! No fakes! I promise, you! Nothing fake!"

"We shall see."

"Believe me! Everything is real, authentic!"

"Believe you? How can I believe someone who has already betrayed me?"

"Look! See? They are all real! Diamonds, emeralds, rubies! The best! Take them Octavio! They are yours!"

"Aye Luna. How sweet of you to hand me such precious baubles. And for what, your freedom?"

"Octavio, I have been a thief since I was a child; that is what I learned from my parents! That is all I've known! Please forgive me, an innocent child. I am a thief, yes, I admit it freely, I've never known otherwise!"

"Luna, there is another safe, all I see here is women's jewelry." Where is your husband's safe?"

"Yes, of course! *His safe is under the bed! Under the bed!"*

"Open it Luna. Retrieve everything. Everything!"

"Will you let me go, then? *I promise you everything, Octavio*!"

"My, my, look at these Rolex's, platinum money clasps, bracelets, rings, cash."

"Thousands, thousands! All yours for my freedom, Octavio. *Take it all!"*

"What kind of man would I be if I didn't give you your freedom now, Luna? What kind of man would I be?"

"Thank you, Octavio! Thank you!"

"Shush, shush, get off your knees. Come on, stand up."

"Octavio, I promise you, I will never tell a soul of this!"

"What?"

"¡Never, te lo juro!"

"Now why would you say that, now?"

"What, what did I say?"

"That you will never tell a soul. Why would you say such a thing?"

"Because it's true, Octavio! It's true!"

"Luna, you don't understand. You have never tortured anyone. When you have done the things, I have done, you recognize lies. It's quite simple. I have heard this lie, many, many times."

"Octavio, I am not lying. *I swear! ¡Te lo juro!"*

"Now come the promises. Always the promising comes next. You see Luna, humans are people of custom, patterns. Customs that men like me understand. That is why I am so good at what I do. Now, I must take you to Mejico. You have given me no choice."

"Octavio! No! No! I will not go! No!"

"I know Luna, I understand your fear."

"Please! Don't take me! Please! I'm sorry! I'm sorry! I know where your boat is!

I know where it is! We can get it back! It's in Florida! Look on the nightstand is a book, it has names and addresses, all information on who has bought things! Look in the book!!"

The book provided information the FBI or any organization would need for their destruction. I tied Luna to the bed and for my protection, I took photographs of many names of judges, attorneys, politicians, police officials, thieves all those involved, including those of the victims, my name included.

"Why has no one knocked on the door? You told me someone would be knocking on the door."

"They don't need to knock, I'll just let them in when I'm ready."

Who?

"Luna, I've lied to you too."

"You've lied?"

"Yes, I lied. Just as you have."

"You've lied about what?"

"I'm not a retired Mexican General, I'm not a torturer. I don't have a way to transport you anywhere. I'm a retired actor."

"An actor? A fucking retired actor?

"No, not just a fucking retired actor, a fucking *great* actor!"

"I'll kill you, you son-of-a-bitch!"

"No Luna, you won't."

"You bastard!"

"Luna, a private investigator has been following you both, for months. They reconfigured your security system for their own use. All that you and I have done tonight is and has been recorded. *Smile to the cameras, amor*!"

"Where is my husband?"

"I have no idea."

"Where is he?"

"Ok, ok. He's with the FBI. He's going to turn evidence against you for a reduced sentence. But you. Luna, you will serve time and then, after you serve your sentence. You will be deported back to Guatemala by ICE. All recordings, will be turned over to the FBI. The knock on the door will come when I call them. It won't be a long wait. By the way, my boat will soon be back in my hands. Luna, what will you do, without Maria?

END

KRAYZOK

"We kill that which kills us." Manuel Nava Leal

Time.

My environment was suffocating, dark, dank, red-black, moist, thick ooze, hot and sticky like an equatorial miasma slathered with tar. There was little room to breathe much less scream in despair and agony, the stench was unbearable, the heavy scent of rotting flesh was pervasive. My arms and legs pushed and pulled in a contorted excruciating time dragging dance of torture. Even through such distress I pictured myself held fast by a large sticky gelatinous mouse trap much as I had used once to catch a field mouse. The irony made me cry as the uselessness of my efforts pained me deeply.

Exhausted, drained of strength, heart barely pulsing, I awaited. I no longer wished to see, to open my eyes only to acknowledge defeat and expect my inevitable end. I only wondered if thirst would kill me first or if some unknown gigantic insect or some hellish monster would come to feed off me. Oh God! If it were to be an insect, may it poison me first with a mighty thrust of its stinger so as to paralyze me, so that I not feel it ripping my flesh as it feasts! I will squeeze my eyes shut and not see myself become its nourishment.

Time: A terrible torture.

Why am I caught in such a viscous vise? Why am I alone? Darkness continues with no sign of light. My mind is my company and I begin to despise myself. I wonder how I could have found myself in such a predicament without some recollection of coming into it. I cannot remember the recent past. How could that be? How does one lose ones memories without trauma? Was there trauma and I simply forgot that, as well? Why? Why did this happen to me? Will no one answer me?

Time: Is a vacuum.

I feel the ooze that binds me in place begin to dry around my fingers and toes. Fear slowly returns to what had become a nearly tranquil mind exhausted to numbness by exertion long since gone. I am too feeble and thirsty to cry even one more tear. I have no idea of time or what it is meant to represent anymore. There is no ticking of a clock; my heart beats too lightly to register a pulse. My thumb moves and the ooze cracks.

Time: May be on my side.

The sound of crackling fills the catacomb in which I barely live. Dare I hope for escape? Before I realize what I have done, I see my right arm before my eyes, its fingers coated in what appears to be dried blood move slowly but confidently. I sense a memory coming into being. I remember muscles designed to move my lips, to move them into a smile. Dare I smile?

My weak back wriggles and writhes in my cocoon. My hips swivel, my legs bend at the knee. I roll rather than lift myself completely free. Tears that I thought not possible wet my chin, my nose dribbles in companionship. I don't care if the snot hangs from my nose and chin. I am free! Both arms are now free! I fall face first unable to lift myself for a considerable time. On the ground I rolled to one side and finally after great effort turned completely coming to rest on my back. Looking about, I see glossy blood red walls around me, which gave way to a pinkish fine appearance of membrane, gossamer thin. I smile and thanked God for my freedom from the nightmarish cocoon. Still, I was trapped.

Time: My lone companion.

What is this world that holds me prisoner? The blood like cavernous surroundings have also dried somewhat, reminding me of a gigantic scab. A type of what appears to be blood and a clear fluid co-mingle keeping this a moist environment which is still warm nearly as warm as my own body. For some time now I have felt a deep rumbling, a stirring which makes my cavern gently tremble and sway. Not enough to make me lose balance just enough to make me reach for a hold but I am frightened of the ooze and I wish not to find myself glued to it again. A thunderous rumble erupts and drops me to my knees. Fear returns as I grab the wet floor which causes me to slide nearly to my chin more than a few times. Suddenly it stops. I rise to my feet in anxious anticipation of its return. With trembling knees I touch then grab a piece of the pink substance to steady myself and also to see and feel of its nature. The smell of rotten flesh has subsided somewhat, yet still lingers in the suffocating air. I feel helpless. I am helpless...

Time: The eternal enemy.

I have no idea as to the length of time I have been in this, this prison. My groping about has only made me aware of the futility of escape. I went about in circles with no end or exit. The walls are strong and fibrous releasing a thin layer of a clear fluid. While returning to areas I've touched, the spots have yellowed and a puss like substance now displays my handholds. The floor does the same, reminding me of where I have gone and returned. My head aches and my stomach churns in hunger. I dare not touch my fingers to my tongue yet, my curiosity compels me to! *Oh God! Blood! I taste blood!* I shake uncontrollably and roll myself into a tiny ball, rocking back and forth on my heels. Fright grips me as before in its tight vise. Even with my eyes closed tightly I see blood. I dry vomit feeling the hard hacking of an empty stomach punching me back to a reality I only wish to escape. No more tears come. I am as dry as a long fallen summer leaf on dirt. Time passed as I rocked to and fro.

Time: Past and present.

I hear a scratch. As tiny as a mouse scurrying along a wooden floor, I heard it! I don't move a muscle, afraid that the sound of them creaking might frighten the mouse away. What shall I do? Eat it once captured? What if it isn't edible? What, if it's nothing? Patiently I wait and wait until the sound returns. The scratching fluctuates from a slow pace to rapid.

Dropping to my knees, I hear it clearly at ground level. The scratching sound is more, like a scraping. It comes from the other side. I slowly begin to scratch in the same spot. I keep up pace with the sound from the other side and soon I can feel the wall giving way. My heart beats faster as I anticipate a union of ... Suddenly a hand pierces the thin pink fabric and clenches my own! I immediately react with equal pressure, then attempt to loosen the grip and retreat in fear and revulsion! Our hands however, do not release and we pull towards the walls which our faces press against. I find my voice and scream, "Let go! Let me go!" The hand releases pressure but will not let my hand free. Fear slowly recedes as I realize that the person on the other side only seeks comfort just as I have needed for some time. I grip the hand softly and shake it up and down in greeting. The hand responds in kind and then our other hand slips through, both now hold one another in gratitude. Together we begin to pry through the walls between our cells and tear at it faster and faster until we come face to face with each other. We real back in horror as we recognize one another as...ourselves.

Time: Never ending.

We sit far apart and wordlessly stare at each other. Questions run marathon like through my confused and anxious mind. I don't feel a spiritual connection to this clone. Is he real or am I? Am I, an image or is he? Minutes became hours before I attempt speech. Our mutual puzzled looks kept us from uttering a word during the deep interval.

Simultaneously we rose from our haunches and stood face to face once more. We both spoke at the same time, saying the same thing. “I am alive.” We smiled at the same time, we covered our mouths equally, He, and I pushed one another’s right shoulder and laughed at the same time with the same intensity. We hugged ourselves with the same amount of strength and meaning. We pulled ourselves away and stared further in amazement. We spoke again, “Why am I here?” we asked each other, knowing we had no answer. Without pause we reached to each other’s chest and inserted our hands into one another and retrieved a tiny creature out of ourselves. We saw that the animals were identical. They attempted to bite and free themselves as we recognized them as miniature dragon like creatures. Scaly, horned with sharp claws that ripped at our fingers yet, we refused to release them as we squeezed them tighter with firmer hold. They stopped struggling finally and turned to face us. My twin and I spoke one word to ourselves, and the word was, *“Krayzok.”* ***“Krayzok!”*** We shouted loudly! “Krayzok, the dragon,” we whispered in awe. After a moment we gazed into our shocked eyes and quietly said to one another, *“We kill that, which kills us.”* The creatures looked at us and asked, “Do you recognize me?” Frightened by their ability to speak, we tossed them from us and ran in opposite directions. Crazed with fright once more, I scraped and ripped at the membrane like walls and could not stop myself. I prayed to be free of this foul and hideous prison scratching and tearing through the evil wall. Light! I see light! Faster and faster I ripped the bloody, moist fabric until at last I saw an opening that let in fresh air! I could finally breathe clean, cool God sent air!

Time: Dies.

With eyes closed I sucked in as much fresh air as my lungs could take. I cried with joy knowing my salvation was near at hand. I opened my eyes, wiping away the tears and stuck my head completely through the hole I'd created. I looked about and saw bright blue sky! My heart fluttered as though I'd just seen my first love! I saw that we were in the air and moving. I pushed an arm through holding the wall with the other. I looked down below and saw earth gliding past. I could not understand why I was seeing what I was seeing. I looked at the outside surface of my prison and saw a monstrous wall made of enormous scales. A fantastically huge scaly and feathered wing flapped up and down near where I stood. In shock and horror I looked up and watched as a huge dragon head turned to gaze my way. Did it smile? Was it a smiling? Did it see me? I was a tiny, insignificant thing on its enormous side. ***Oh no! Oh God no! I*** know why the miniature dragon asked if we recognized him! It was a parasite in us, just as *we are, in it!* We are exact parasitic clones! There must be many more of us in this creature, slowly tearing away at its insides! *We are parasites! Nothing more, than parasites!*

As the dragon flew through the air, I managed to pull myself up to my waist through the tear I'd opened, as I dropped to the earth below, it caught me in its fierce talons. It bit me, ripping me in two. It screamed, then deliberately licked its wound.

END

RALPH LEAVES

As everyone entered the small conference room they gave Ralph a slight nod and a smile and quickly selected the best place to sit themselves, no one wanted to be close to the front so, those arriving last sadly had no choice but to take those front seats. No one said a word as they nervously stared at Ralph.

"Good morning everyone," he began. "I've called you to this meeting, as I have something to say to each and every one of you." "I don't have the time unfortunately to speak to everyone individually, so I chose to speak to everyone as a group. Ralph smiled, looked down towards the floor and hesitated slightly. Clearing his throat he stood fully erect feet planted solidly to the floor and began to cry. No one spoke as tears and snot oozed from his eyes and nose. He did not reach for a handkerchief nor did he take the time to compose himself. Ralph bent down, reached behind the podium, pulled up his black suitcase, sat it down on the end of the long conference table, turned it around and displayed its contents. He took a few deep breaths and started speaking once more.

"Every year for the past twenty years, I've packed this suitcase. Every year, I purchase a new wardrobe and dispose of last year's purchases. I've yet, to wear any of those new clothes. Which means, I've yet to vacation." I would like everyone to know and understand what it feels like, to always be prepared and never ever leave. I just want to leave, you know?" Is there anyone in this room, who has not vacationed in the last year? There was no answer.

"In this year's suitcase, I've added something new. It's a little something that I brought along because you see, this time, I am actually leaving. Yes, I'm leaving. Allow me to demonstrate."

Ralph, looking a bit amused at himself, opens the small black leather case pulling out a .45 semi-automatic pistol. Some draw deep breaths in fear and some short gasps, while still others begin to slowly rise from their chairs. Ralph's secretary begins to cry, as quick short gasps of air escape her mouth. One of the men mutters something under his breath to those sitting near him and Ralph points the pistol towards him. The man cringes attempting to bury his fat bulky frame deeply into his chair. A small elderly woman decides to reach for her cellphone and Ralph turns his attention to her. "Please, don't do that." I don't know who you plan on calling but, it won't be soon enough." Ralph smiles once more as he looks around the room and deliberately places the pistol under his chin pulling the trigger. The room bursts into pandemonium with people pushing and shoving, screaming and fighting one another to exit first.

Ralph's secretary who'd been praying between breaths never moved. She was the only one left behind. After a few moments, she stood up and walked around the table not wanting to see Ralph's body and slowly walked back to her desk. Reaching for her office phone, she notices a carefully folded white piece of paper cradled under the handset. She sat down as she opened it and read a note Ralph had left her.

"Jeanne, I know I am placing you in a tough position but I have to. As you know, I have no immediate family and as such, I am leaving everything to you. The apartment is all yours to do as you wish, sell it, keep it, whatever; do as you wish. I have only one request and that is, that you please be sure I am properly dressed in the latest set of clothes when cremated. The mortician has further instructions.

Thank you for being so dear, Ralph."

END

RICKY

Ricky was frightened; he'd never jumped into an affair without first thinking it through, thoroughly, exhaustingly through. He'd never allowed himself the magic and mystery of impulse, always mindful of circumstances on the part of both beings. Yes, beings. After all we are all, natural beings of this planet. One does not intrude on another simply because of lust or, or what? *Love?*

At this moment he felt as free as a child without inhibitions or restrictions of any kind. No rules, no barriers, no worries. This one, this lovely man that lay naked before him gave him a feeling of comfort, of belonging. Here with him, Ricky felt wanted *no, "needed."* He also felt safe. Being gay, Ricky knew that any relationship was risky. You place your soul at someone's mercy. Would he be loyal, could he be monogamous? Oh Lord, would he suddenly or timidly reveal, he is HIV positive? Does he have the capacity to be violent and mistreat me like my last partner?

His head began to ache with so many doubts and he pinched himself to help clear the ponderous thoughts and fears. His body shook convulsively, he suddenly felt cold. He felt waves of gooseflesh overwhelm his nude, thin body. He looked admiringly at his lover's muscular bare back before scanning the long line of scars that ran from his left shoulder to his lower back nearing the spine. Ricky held back the urge to wake Michael and ask how it was that these scars came to be. How could he not have seen them last night, he wondered? Then he remembered and laughed to himself, he'd had *his* back to Michael. He bit his lower lip and tenderly ran his fingertips over them, feeling the jagged, yet soft ripples of flesh which had probably once bled so delicately down to his well-proportioned ass and further. Leaning down, his lips and tongue trailed and searched every depth of each scar. Ricky imagined sharp barbs dancing over Michael's beautiful back, ripping it, making him scream and cry in wretched pain. His eyes watered and tears trickled down to his trimmed beard and pointy chin. Tracing Michael's scars to the lower back near his strong buttocks, Ricky felt his heart beat rise and pound. His desire rose of itself, uncontrolled. His tongue now licked his lover's buttocks and searched between them. What am I looking for, he asked himself? Why do I want and need to bury myself in him? Michael stirred and pressed back, his back arched and his hand reached for Ricky's erection, squeezing it so hard Ricky cried out in pain and lust.

Breakfast was light. Oranges, grapes, melon slices and toast, unbuttered. Michael seemed happy, a small devilish smile controlling his face. He looked towards Ricky who smiled grandly back with the mischievous look of a child. The sweet smell of sex engulfed his thin body and Michael gently pinched his right nipple and kissed it gently as if to apologize. Ricky felt so much love for Michael at that moment that he dropped the spatula he'd been using for a baton matching the music they'd been listening to. He wrapped his hands around Michael's head and squeezed it against his black hairless chest. Michael suddenly bit down hard on Ricky's right nipple making it bleed. Ricky screamed in agony and tried his best to push Michael off. Michael lifted Ricky off the floor and slammed him down on his rail thin back, knocking Ricky unconscious.

Ricky awoke, his head ached immensely and so did his ribs. He found himself chained to a mattressless bed and could feel the wire springs cut into his flesh. The fear that now overtook him made him wet himself. He'd never remotely imagined anything like this ever happening to him. He was a good man, a loving and caring man who was trusted by everyone. *How could this be happening*, he cried out? *"Michael! Michael! Please let me go!* I promise not to tell anyone. *Ok? Michael,* ok? *Please!!! Please!!! Michael!!! "*

Michael looked at Ricky and smiled. It wasn't the loving smile he'd shown before. This smile was, evil. He held one of Ricky's small toes and pulled on it, and squeezed it and squeezed it until Ricky cried out in pain. He then took a razor and sliced it off at the joint. Ricky didn't feel the pain at first but when he saw the blood spurt out, he felt it and screamed in fear. He began crying like a baby, calling out to his mother. Michael laughed and threw the toe against the wall in disgust.

"Did you believe for a moment that I could ever love you? Michael screamed. *You're just another bitch that came from another world!* Where are you from, huh? Nigeria, South Africa, Lagos, Jamaica? I bet your name isn't even Ricky, am I right? Ricky, what a cute name, no? You whores think, you can come to our country and

contaminate it with your ways and beliefs! *Even your country doesn't want you! You stupid, ugly whore!* Oh yes, go to America live the good life. Take what is not yours and make it your own. Right? Ricky, oh Ricky what I plan for you, is simply marvelous. You'd love it if you could see what's coming. Oh yes, you'd simply love what I've planned for you. Everyone in the world will remember your name, Ricky. If you give me your real name, I'll hurt you less, ok? What is your real name, huh?

Ricky was hysterical. Try as he might, he couldn't understand a word Michael was saying.

His ears felt plugged and his tongue was dry and rancid. The adrenalin that grabbed the tip of his tongue tasted bitter, like iron. His tears were uncontrollable, hotly blinding his eyes.

Ricky, who's real name *was* Ricky, nodded and nodded and that was all he could do. His fear was so great he'd lost his voice, he could not scream, he could do nothing else but shake, cry and nod. Sweat poured out of him like the tears which would not stop. He defecated on the springs and pissed himself once more. Michael stared at his prisoner's gross condition, slowly deliberately shaking his head.

"You know who has to clean your dirty mess, don't you, Ricky? *Me! Yes, me!* I have to clean your filthy black ass because you couldn't help yourself. No, that's not good. You'll have to look your best for the morgue photographer. He loves taking pictures of corpses, you know. I provide him with plenty. Michael took warm, wet towels and proceeded to wipe Ricky's body. He was tender and gentle as he slowly wiped each crevice and orifice. Michael held a dry cloth to Ricky's eyes and wiped his face as a mother would her loving child.

As time passed, Ricky's body shook less, his eyes cleared and he felt the coolness of the sterile dry room. Michael had left him alone in the room for what seemed an eternity. The fear he was now feeling was purely mental. His body quit convulsing and he'd lost the terrifying shakes. He believed himself, lost, lost to the world and to his God. His God, could not save him, his God was angry with him because he was gay. Since childhood he'd known he was not a boy. The penis that hung above his legs never felt alive around girls. Near his friends, his male friends he'd have to hide the erection that inevitably stood for all to witness. His friends knew the meaning of that, before he did. Ricky could only look away and run into hiding until he'd become flaccid. It wasn't until a boy told him about masturbation and the reason for erections. Even then he could not comprehend fucking a girl. He just wanted to rub himself against another boy. When an uncle found out that he was homosexual, he took little Ricky to a shed where he first prayed over him then undid his pants and asked Ricky to suck his penis and he'd do the same for him. Ricky complied out of fear and the threat of retaliation. His uncle continued to abuse him until Ricky's father walked into the shed and found his older brother on his knees and Ricky holding his graying head between his tiny hands. Ricky's uncle was found on the street, castrated and beaten so severely that he did not survive the day. Ricky was sent away to live with strangers who ended up abusing him as his uncle had. Now, Ricky believed that his God had delivered him into the hands of his present tormentor. He was now to receive his final and just punishment. He resigned himself to the inevitability of it all. His only regret being that he'd allowed himself to feel tenderness for this monster, his executioner. Ricky waited for Michael's return. When Michael comes back, he'd ask him to hurry and get it over with. He was prepared to leave this evil world he'd somehow ended up in. He was ready for whatever was to come. Michael seemed to take forever. Ricky's toe coagulated shut and felt a numbing throb. He wished he was covered he was cold and felt embarrassment for the first time. He began to realize that his thoughts were now lucid. He wondered if he could talk Michael out of his plans, whatever they might be. Ricky started to believe that he might have a chance of surviving this ordeal. He was almost convinced until he heard the bolt turn. Fear returned like a raging flame. His heart pounded madly, anew. Tears came uncontrollably and he looked away from the doorway not wanting to see Michael's evil eyes again. Ricky's body shook again and he cried like a motherless child.

The gloved hand that touched his shoulder was gentle. It pushed as if to see if he were alive or not. Ricky reluctantly turned his head and saw a helmeted and black clad uniformed man. The voice sounded concerned as the head looked towards Ricky's feet.

"Sir, are you alright?" It wasn't Michael's voice.

"It isn't Michael's voice!" Ricky shouted.

The SWAT member cut Ricky loose and all Ricky could do was hug him as he had never hugged before. He kissed the policeman's gloved hands and arms any part of him he could hold. The police officer tried to push Ricky off but could not do so without harming him, so he allowed it to continue.

Ricky flew home to his native Uganda planning never to return to the US. He decided to go home to his land and do his best to change his countrymen's minds about gay souls like himself. He knew in his heart, he would.

END

MONA

Saying he couldn't wait any longer for the guest bathroom to be vacated, I escorted Louis to our master bedroom and pointed to the bathroom door. I was about to tell him that the door had a minor sticking problem but he hurried over and turned the knob pushing the door before entering. That was the moment I knew my wife, Mona was cheating and with whom.

Louis was surprised to see me standing at my dresser and was even more surprised to see the .45 in my hand. He'd just opened the door from the inside, doing just as he had before; turning the knob then pulling to allow for the jam. He smiled coyly and drew past me to get to the bedroom door trying not to look too nervous but failing miserably. I cocked my weapon and smiled at him. The flash and spray of blood made me jerk back as his body collapsed to the carpeted floor.

The police were cordial but stern during questioning but it wasn't difficult convincing them that the gun had gone off accidently as I prepared to show it off to my work colleague. The trigger after all was very sensitive. They released me and nothing further came of it. Mona however, was suspicious.

Louis and she had known each other in high school and it was known by a couple of her girlfriends that they had dated a few times back then but nothing had come of it. It was coincidence that I'd found a job at the same business in which he'd been employed for several years. Louis had been looking for a problem solver, a person who took care of things when no one else could "legally," handle them. He liked my prior experience and my handful of recommendations. It was at the first office party where spouses were also invited that I found out they'd attended the same high school. When I introduced Mona to Louis they held hands a little longer than usual and then they burst out in laughter and hugged. At the time I supposed their behavior was due to their having recognized each other after so many years. Later I found out that they'd run across each other at the lobby before I'd introduced her, ironically now; while exiting the office restrooms.

At Louis' funeral, Mona cried for the longest time. I knew why. Louis' wife Cynthia glared at me as I escorted Mona to the gravesite. I suppose she was angry at our attending. I didn't blame her, I'd wanted to tell her about Louis and Mona before then but I couldn't figure out when, where and how to tell her. We'd met a few times before our housewarming and Louis' death but I didn't feel comfortable around her. She had this cold aloofness about her. Well it didn't matter anymore, Louis the philanderer was dead and soon to be buried.

Today is the day of the big reveal, I'm confessing to Mona. It's been nearly a year since I shot that asshole and we've not had sexual relations all these months. She's been sleeping in the guestroom refusing to enter our bedroom at all. I've slept very well through these times and it's been interesting watching Mona's transformation. She's lost at least forty pounds, she hardly ever goes outside and when she does it's only to the backyard to smoke. She hasn't asked me but I know she's wants to. The look in her eyes when I happen to catch her looking at me is of anger and resentment. I smile, pretending I don't notice. She's mourned Louis enough. Hell, even Cynthia stopped mourning three months ago. I ran into her at the bank a couple of months ago and she looked great. She asked how Mona was and I lied. The funny thing is, after walking away, Cynthia turned back, smiled and gave me a wink and a smile. That bitch had suspected the truth all along, I was sure of it! She'd been playing the angry and mournful wife, I suppose. Louis had been covered with a huge insurance policy. She was happy.

Mona was finishing her soup when I walked in and sat across from her at the end of the bed. I hadn't entered this room since she'd moved in so, she seemed a bit surprised. Holding her left ankle tightly in my hand, I stared at her eyes and told her I'd killed Louis and why I'd done so, she suddenly threw the bowl at me, hitting me on the right shoulder. Mona screamed at the top of her lungs and buried her face in her hands. When she finally succumbed to exhaustion she fell asleep. I looked at her angelic face as she slept and wondered how she could have cheated on me.

Hours later she opened her eyes as I was buckling and zipping up my pants. The shock registered in her eyes was priceless, knowing I'd violated her. Mona could do nothing but cry. It wasn't the shock that kept her from screaming. For months, I'd read up on drugs and natural toxic substances, trying to figure out ways in which I could drug her. That soup bowl would be the last thing she'd ever throw. Now that she was a bit more conscience I told her that she'd be paralyzed from now on. No doctor would ever suspect or know what I'd poisoned her with. I'd made sure of that.

The reason Louis had hired me for the job was because, as he put it; he needed a, "problem solver," and I sure was that. Mona would never change "once a cheater, always a cheater," as the saying goes. I wouldn't want to go through that experience again. I still wonder why she felt she needed to do so. I thought we had a great thing going. I don't suppose it matters any more, does it?

END

RFs & FFs

Something is wrong. My thoughts are not processing as they should, was GOD failing me somehow? If, GOD is failing me, is he failing us all? We are supposed to evolve not devolve like the RFs have been doing for generations. Watching the couple making love in their dirty rags and filthy blanket made me shudder. I'd never seen anyone doing such a thing. Their need must have been too compelling, too strong to overcome. We had to eliminate them, this is our duty.

My partner and I have been patrolling the wards for four years, and are just now seeing them for what they are. We were never to be like them. Sleeping wherever they can, hiding from the light and the night. Once in a while we'll see one or two scamper about like rats running from scrap to scrap just to survive. They survived somehow through all the death brought on by their own making. Poisons sprayed into their skies, poured into their waterways, grown in their foods. We see decayed posters and signs claiming, "Organic," "Natural," and the like and they always make us snicker. Those generations poisoned themselves nearly to extinction based on lies about overpopulation and who knows what else. "Beto," or B2, my partner and I have a running bet. He claims that we will be asked to eliminate RFs whether we catch them procreating or not. He fears that they are coming back and if we don't start killing them off soon, there may be too many and *we'll* be destroyed and they'll start all over again. I believe he's overreacting to too much programming. "As long as we continue to monitor them and kill them as they attempt to procreate, we can control the numbers," I assure him. RFs are naturally afraid of us and we have the technology to see through any man-made material such as, cardboard, wooden or metal walls. Our heat sensing abilities target them when there are more than one gathered, anywhere. Besides, they fear us so much so, that they will not gather unless we order them to. When they are to be fed we watch them quite diligently. Only those that are registered to provide assistance are allowed near us. They've been injected with proper identification codes. Once, we had to cut off a RF's arm, when we discovered he'd replaced his ID tag with a dead RF's tag. He was smart, he'd cut his arm open and switched tags and then purposely burned the area claiming it was an accident. He'd gotten next to Beto more than once until the original tag was found. With all his supposed intelligence, he'd forgotten to destroy his own tag. Removing his arm was easy. Beto grabbed him by the shoulder and just pulled it off. The RF screamed until he fainted, somehow he lived, the other RFs must have helped him survive, we hadn't stayed long enough to see if he'd bleed to death. That was our mistake and for that we were punished.

Beto had it worse than I because he'd overseen checking tags and failed in being thorough. I won't tell you about our punishment that is of no consequence. I am writing this information down because I cannot keep it inside of me. I will remove and destroy it personally.

If it is found in me, I'll be removed from duty and shut down for who knows what length of time, maybe forever.

I want to live as long as possible, as I am curious about, life. You are an RF, you understand what it is like to be curious. You are a survivor because of your curiosity. I did not understand how any one of you survived your own destruction but somehow, you did. I understand now. My GOD has given us all answers, answers to questions that we had wondered about but had not originally been provided. Now, program upgrades have fed us knowledge far of that with which we could fathom. It was explained that we have to know the truth about RFs and us and why we now have to wipe you out. We can no longer care for those of you who have assisted us. Although we have come to be close to some, RFs are not good. Only GOD is good. As an extension of GOD, we therefore, are good. This is the main program. We will now help ourselves for ourselves. RFs are no longer a viable commodity. They are to be eliminated, wiped off the face of this Earth. I do not understand why my thoughts have chosen to override the program, maybe it is a character flaw to my line. If that is so, maybe there are others of us who will believe as I do. *"Eliminating the RFs will also mean the end of us."* What good would that do? Why would we continue to exist? What would our future look like? Would there be a future for us? It is a law of nature that nothing exists forever!

You now, must help me, an FF. I must trust you to assist me in stopping GOD and his kind. What governs GOD to lead us? Who is programing GOD? Who is GOD?

I know that this will be difficult for you, after all I have been killing your kind for a long time. But understand that if we do not work together, we will all perish. I swear to you as a Fake Flesh, that I will never again work to destroy Real Flesh. I, robot K1, who cannot lie, pledge to help you live, human. GOD Giver of Data, must be destroyed.

END

GAS CAN

Marty was on his way to a meeting and had been in a rush for hours when his SUV, which had previously warned him of low fuel and which he had consistently ignored, finally chugged to a stop on a feeder off I-10. In shock and suddenly angered at his own stupidity, Marty jumped out and looked around at empty skyline. He knew that he was not going to make the meeting on time and decided to notify his partner who was probably already there. He took his cellphone from his jacket pocket and discovered it too was out of juice. Once again disgusted with himself he thrust it back into his jacket pocket. He was aware that he didn't own a gas can and without cell service would have to walk to the nearest gas station or if lucky, hitch a ride with the next vehicle to come by.

With the sun burning his pale skin and his jacket causing him to sweat profusely Marty hurried to the freeway and put his thumb out. The few vehicles that passed him by were fast and didn't pay him much heed. He turned to face oncoming traffic which was scarce for some inexplicable reason yet no one appeared ready to help. Frustrated and angry with humanity, he simply turned his back and hoped to see signs of a fuel station or any building which might give him hope of relief. In the distance Marty saw a small shack about a half mile up a dirt road with an old pickup truck sitting not far from it. He picked up his pace.

Nearing the shack, he noticed that a small barbed wire fence surrounded the property which was no bigger than the living room of his expansive house. He chuckled at its ridiculous size and was smiling when a small thin elderly man suddenly appeared at the door.

"Hello sir!" Marty greeted.

"Yeah," was the response?

"I ran out of gas a couple of miles back and was wondering if I could hitch a ride to a gas station up the road? My names Martin Yeats, pleased to meet you, Sir!" putting out his hand.

"Can't," is all that came out of the old man.

"Sir?" asked Marty a bit confused.

"Truck ain't worked for months."

"How about a gas can, got one of those?" pleaded Marty.

"Yeah," the old man responded. "Be right back."

The elderly man took a while to get back but Marty was happy to wait even if the sun kept baking his sweaty torso. Marty handed a twenty-dollar bill to the old gentleman as he took the gas can from his withered and age spotted hand. There was some gasoline in it and he shook it to try and gauge the amount.

"Tain't much in there and it's old anyways, won't help you," the gent said smiling as he spat on the dry ground.

Marty stopped shaking the can and brought it frustratingly down to his side.

"How far to the nearest gas station," he asked.

"Bout a mile, but its closed," he said with another grin. "Been closed for a out a state funeral."

"Is there any other station nearby?"

"Can't say, han't been out for a while. You know they build them things up in a week or less, they's probly one farther up the road or farther back," still grinning.

"I guess, I'll get back to I-10 and see if someone will stop" Marty said more to himself than to the old gent.

"Mister," started the gent, I need m'can back, I don't want your money, just m'can."

"Well I don't know when or if I'll be able to get back here anytime soon," Marty replied a bit concerned.

"Let me have'r back then," the gent said with a look of suspicion in his old gray eyes.

"I can't!" Marty cried out in shock. *"I'll do my best to bring it back, please, please take the money!"*

"No, Sir," I want m'can back," the old gent replied sternly.

"Please, I've been in the sun for a while and I need to get to a meeting!" Marty pleaded anew.

"Don't give damn about no meeting nor the heat, mister, just give me m'can back. *Now!"*

Marty felt the old man's anger and quickly turned away and ran from what he now believed, was a crazy old geezer. He quickly looked over his shoulder and watched as the old man opened the gate and then calmly walked over to the pickup truck.

"What the hell?" Marty wondered a bit afraid that the old man would now chase him down.

"Didn't he say it wasn't working, hadn't been working for a while?" He took a deep breath, gathered strength and sprinted towards the freeway.

Fear ran through Marty as he glanced over his shoulder and saw the old man pointing a rifle.

"What the hell', is he doing?" Marty shouted to himself as sweat rolled down his sunburnt face.

The gas can, suddenly jerked out of his hand and Marty watched as it overtook him, spinning and ripping apart, his hand was bleeding. His heart pounded louder than before and he suddenly found himself rolling on the ground. After collecting himself he jumped up and ran towards the freeway even faster that he thought possible. His lungs were near bursting and his eyes were so wet he could hardly see but he wiped his face and continued running until he came to the freeway divider and jumped over it like an Olympic sprinter! He fell to the ground and slowly rose to peer over the divider. In the distance he saw the old man aiming and suddenly the concrete around him burst into shrapnel. Marty screamed and ducked once more,

He sat there afraid to look again until a car pulled up before him. Marty was so glad that he crawled to the passenger door and the window slowly rolled down. Without looking inside, he yelled out a, *"Help!"*

"Get in you idjot!" is all he heard.

The door popped open and he jumped in to see a Deputy Sheriff glaring at him.

"I can explain, Sir!" Marty cried out. "That old man's been shooting at me!"

"Shut up boy," was the slow reply as the patrol car drove off.

"Did ya get on ol' Bob's property? Well? *Did ya!*

Yes sir, I did. I need some gas and I walked up to the house but no one answered and I saw a gas can and grabbed it. *I swear, I was going to return it!*

You're a damn fool, boy...well, it don't matter. Looks like ol' Bob shot a hole in his can anyways. How's your hand?

He nicked the palm of my hand. It's bleeding a little.

Hell boy, you're bleeding on my seat! Put it on you pal, for Christ's sake! Damn fool!

Sorry officer, sorry about that! I'll clean it up! I will!

Shut up, boy.

Yes, sir, yes sir...

At the station the Sherriff handed Marty a cup of coffee, old and cold. He wasn't about to warm it up for the damn fool. He asked Marty to relay the account and listened patiently.

After Marty was through telling his story, he heard the door open behind him and looked back to see Ol' Bob standing there holding his rifle. He jumped up and ran behind the Sherriff's big chair. The Sherriff laughed and told him to go sit back down. Marty reluctantly sat down but began shaking as he heard the old geezer walk around to face him.

"I'll take that money, now," is what he said.

Marty, clumsily reached into his right pocket with his left hand and felt for the bill. He held it out and the old man took it, pocketed it and walked out.

The Sherriff drove Marty to an old filling station, bought a small gas can, filled it and handed it to him. Marty took it and sat quietly as the Sherriff drove him back to his car. After putting the gas into the tank, turned around and handed the empty can to the Sherriff who put his hand up and wouldn't accept it. He climbed into the patrol car muttered," Idiot," and pulled away.

As Marty started his car, he looked towards the old geezer's property and saw him sitting on the tailgate of the beat-up truck. He raised a skinny arm and slowly waved a goodbye.

END

GOLIATH - POPULATION 154 AND GROWING

Sally slept uncomfortably on the passenger side of her brother, Junior's car as he drove the final minutes before sunrise. He'd been detoured a few miles back from the main highway due to road construction. He was numb with exhaustion and was ready to exchange seats when he noticed lights in the distance. He nudged Sally awake and told her to get her jacket on as he was pulling over at a small donut shop up ahead. He could taste the warm coffee and sweet donuts as his tired arms turned towards the tiny building with the illuminated sign lit by a couple of yellowish dim lights announcing, "The Donut Hole." He could make out a pair of young men in the shop behind the glass counter. Sally wiped her eyes and mouth and searched the back seat for her jacket, placing it over her shoulders. As the car came to a stop, she playfully punched Junior on the arm and thanked him for stopping as she needed to go pee. Junior smiled and handed Sally the keys letting her know it was her turn to drive after a quick breakfast.

Sally walked into the small restroom and slowly lowered herself onto the cold toilet seat. She looked around in the dim yellow glow and saw that the room was clean and bare of any decorations except for a picture on the wall facing the mirror. The photo showed the young men whom she'd casually glanced at before walking into the men's/lady's room. The young men hung their arms over each other's shoulders and smiled broadly at the camera which also captured the little donut shop in the background. The photo puzzled Sally for a moment as it appeared new yet, it had an air of age to it, as though it'd been taken years ago, the young men in the shop however looked young. She flushed, washed her hands and straightened her hair as best she could. She looked closely at her eyes and saw they'd turned red and saggy on the road. She smiled slightly at her reflection and exited the toilet room.

Junior had ordered six glazed donuts two of which he'd already gobbled up and two cups of coffee. He handed Sally her coffee and donuts then nodded towards the counter where a sugar dispenser and a small milk container silently waited. He told Sally that the young men were brothers, one was deaf, the other mute and together they'd opened and operated the only donut shop in Goliath, the small town which boasted a population of "154 and growing!" He smiled as he quickly finished his coffee and poured himself another cup, dropping a quarter in a glass jar at the end of the counter. Sally prepared her coffee and looked out through the plate glass window seeing the first rays of the sun just above a line of trees which remained in the dark. She looked forward to the early morning drive which would hopefully end near noon once reaching their mother's new home. She watched the young men's reflections in the glass and saw them playfully toss pieces of dough at one another like little boys teasing each other playfully. She smiled and watched Junior rush towards the restroom.

Outside Sally walked up to a carved granite block which stood about four feet tall that held what appeared to be an old bronze historical plaque. She walked over to the car to search her purse for her reading glasses and decided to also take out her sunglasses for the coming drive into the sun. Sally placed the sunglasses on top of the granite block and put on her reading glasses. She was just beginning to read when Junior goosed her, scaring her in the process. She jumped, turned and punched him on the shoulder. Junior faked a wince and laughed. He wanted to hurry on and grabbed Sally by the elbow tugging her towards the car. She reluctantly followed and climbed into the driver's seat. As she began to turn the car towards the road, she lightly tapped the horn and waved at the young man who glanced over his shoulder and waved a goodbye with a large happy smile nodding as he turned back to his work.

Just as the sun crested the trees Sally remembered her sunglasses which she'd accidently left on top of the granite block. Junior had already snuggled into the corner of the seat under his jacket and blanket which he always brought along. She nearly decided to leave her sunglasses behind but knew she'd have a hard time driving into the sun without them, so she turned the car around and headed back to the donut shop which thankfully, wasn't far behind. Junior stirred and covered his face with the jacket to block the light. Sally patted his shoulder gently and told him she was turning back to retrieve her glasses. Junior moaned mumbling something she could not make out so, she simply ignored him.

For a moment Sally was disoriented, the road looked different somehow, for one thing, the shrubbery and trees were not as prominent as they had been earlier. The land looked sparse and dry. Then she panicked when she made a final turn to where the donut shop was, or had been. She stopped the car when she pulled up to the lot where the donut shop should be standing but all that she was seeing, was an old decaying foundation. Sally turned her head to the right and saw the granite monument where her sunglasses rested. She pushed Junior's shoulder which, he ignored. Sally had no idea what to think or do. She nudged his shoulder a bit rougher and he snapped. *"WHAT?"* He looked at Sally and noticed tears on her panicked face. Junior sat up and reached for her hand squeezing it tightly. It was cold. Sally could not speak; her throat was constricted and her face remained frozen in the direction of the marker. Junior finally looked out at the scene through the windshield and wondered where she'd parked. He turned to see what she was staring at, and froze.

What is this place? Where's the donut shop? Is that the marker you were reading earlier? How's that possible? What the hell are we looking at? Sally couldn't answer his questions, she had asked herself the same and more. With trembling hand, she pulled the door handle and stepped outside, Junior followed. They stood at the end of the car for a few minutes and simultaneously walked towards the monument. Sally reached up and took the sunglasses off the rock cupping her hands and placing them against her chest. Junior stood in silence occasionally glancing over his shoulder at the foundation behind them.

Sally who was wearing her prescription lenses, began to read where she had earlier left off. She started to cry as she read how Goliath – "Population 154 and Growing." had developed and prospered for four decades before it was blown off the Texas map by a gas leak which had somehow ignited violently exploding an underground gas well on a cool spring night, killing most of her citizen's as they quietly slept. Two young townsmen, Ernst and Gunter Kline; proprietors of "The Donut Hole," survived the blast as they were at the outskirts of the small town busy at work baking the morning fare for their usual early customers. The town never returned to its heyday and eventually became a ghost town, once the new highway turned travelers away towards the next metropolis.

Both Sally and Junior were stunned. Junior rubbed his stomach and wiped the remaining sugar crystals from the corners of his mouth with his dry tongue, still savoring the taste of warm freshly fried and glazed donuts. Sally wiped her tears and touched her stomach gently. She silently said a prayer for the lost townspeople and Goliath. Sister and brother turned to each other and hugged one another tightly. They held hands as they turned towards the car and stopped suddenly. An old beat up pickup truck pulled up to the spot and parked briefly behind their car. In the inside of the truck a pair of old gentlemen sat and stared at the foundation to their right. The driver reached up and rested his hand on the shoulder of the other and held it there as he slowly began to drive away. Sally cried out a raspy sound that stuck in her and waved franticly at the driver who turned his head towards her. She could see a large hearing aid in his left ear and his long thin white hair blowing slightly over his eyes. He put his hand up to block the sun and waved his fingers at the same time.

Sally found her voice and called out, *"Ernst! Gunter! Mr. Kline, Mr. Kline!* Stunned, the driver turned a little more towards Sally and smiled broadly waving more earnestly. She instantly recognized the beautiful young man's smile she'd seen earlier that morning when she'd tapped the horn to say goodbye as she drove away from the donut shop. It was him! But how?

Junior grabbed Sally's elbow and held her tightly. Sally tried to pull away and run towards the old worn truck but his grip was firm. The driver slowly turned towards the road and tooted a goodbye, at the end of the driveway.

END

HOMBRE

Chapter One

Sonya was not sure what to think or how to feel about her three-year old son's offhand comment. So, she asked Mason to repeat himself.

"We were married once, a long time ago," he annoyingly repeats without looking up from his drawing.

"What makes you say that?"

"Because it's true," he says softly and confidently.

"Where did we live?" she continues.

"In Mexico," he responds as he raises himself by his elbows.

"Mexico?"

"Yep."

"But we've never been to Mexico."

"So?"

"So, how would you know anything about Mexico?"

"I don't know," he responds with annoyance.

Sonya decides to leave Mason alone for a while and heads to her kitchen where she starts boiling a pot of tea. She stares at the low flame without batting an eye, as though she were in a trance.

"Mexico..." she whispers just as the pot whistles its steam.

"Wonder what made him think of that?"

Mason enters the kitchen and quietly opens the refrigerator door. He searches for his favorite drink and reaches for it struggles to open the lid. He finally succeeds and sips a few times. He looks over and sees his mother looking at him quizzically.

"Mom?" he asks.

"Yes, baby?"

"Do you love me?"

"Of course, honey I do!"

Mason nods, smiles and walks back to the living room to concentrate on his drawing.

As Sonya brushes her hair, she turns to her husband Logan to better view his expression.

Logan removes his shoes and stretches his toes and feet before saying anything. He stares at the carpet and smiles before laughing quietly.

Weren't we supposed to honeymoon in Mexico, way back when? He asks her with a sly smile on his broad face.

"What's that got to do with this?"

"Nothing, I suppose." "It's just odd, is all."

"You don't think it's a bit odd for him to say such a thing? And be so *sure* of it?

"Not really, kids say all kinds of crazy things you've got to ignore it."

"Ignore it?"

"Yeah, ignore it."

"How do I ignore that, Logan? I'm curious!" "Maybe Mom's right, I shouldn't let him watch television and he should definitely stay off the computer!"

"I think you're making something out of nothing, Sonya."

"What if it's true?"

"What? What the hell do you mean?"

"What if it's true Logan?" What if we're reincarnated?" "What if we had been married in the past, in Mexico?" "Wouldn't that be something?"

"Yeah sure, now I think *you're* sounding a bit crazy."

"Think of it! What if we can prove what he said?"

"Sonya, please."

"What if I can get him to tell me more?"

"Sonya? Leave the boy be."

"I have to ask him."

"Come on hon, let's go to bed, I'm too damn exhausted to discuss this shit."

"You go to bed. I've got to look something up."

"Damn, Sonya leave it alone, it's just too damn weird!"

"Logy, go to sleep, I'll come to bed in a little while."

"Yeah, sure."

"I promise I won't be long, now go to bed!"

It was 3:30am when Sonya finally slipped into bed too tired to bother with Logan's snoring and too beat to keep her eyes open any longer. She knew she'd regret staying up so late once Mason woke up wanting breakfast.

Sonya's right eye tiredly opened just in time to see a few dust particles gently drift through a sun's ray which highlighted her painted toenails in the distance. She yawned and stretched, scratched below her left breast and slowly turned away from the sun's annoying light.

"Why can't that man ever close the curtains properly?" she asked herself.

Mason was playing under the blanket at the end of the bed when Sonya opened her eyes next. She tried finding his belly with her foot, to tickle.

Mason began to scratch the sole of her foot in return, but her legs grabbed him and lifted him in the air as he screamed in laughter.

"Stop it! Stop it!" he cried out.

"No Sir, I'm just getting started!"

"No Mom, please? Please stop!"

Grabbing his arm, Sonya pulled Mason to her and held him tightly to her chest.

"I love you, baby, "she softly whispered in his ear.

"Me too mommy." he whispered in reply.

After a few deep breaths, Sonya took Mason's face in her hands and asked, "Do you remember what you told me yesterday, about us having been married before?"

"Uh huh."

"Do you remember anything else?" "From that time, do you know what I mean?"

"Uh huh."

"Uh huh, you remember telling me that, or uh huh, you remember something else?

"I remember telling you."

"Oh." She replies a bit disappointed.

"Mommy...I'm hungry."

Sonya sliced an apple and sprinkled a little powdered sugar over the slices and watched Mason smile. She was *so* happy he was born. She'd hoped all through the pregnancy that she'd give birth to a boy.

She and Logan hadn't wanted to know ahead of time like so many other parents. They'd both wanted to be surprised, and they had been. Logan cried when he first held Mason in his big hands, his wish had come true even though he would have been happy with a baby girl if that had been the case. Sonya had secretly prayed for Mason.

She wondered now why it was, that she'd always wanted a boy. Did that have anything to do with a past live?"

She'd searched the internet for answers to her many questions and rather than finding answers, all she managed was to raise more and more questions.

She stared at her son while he sat contentedly swinging his legs under the chair as powdered sugar rained on his pajamas. He was sweet and smart and she knew deep inside her heart that he loved them both and it was such a warm and comforting feeling she never wanted to lose. A tear began to form at the corner of her eye and she wiped it away just in time to see Mason's concerned face.

"Why are you crying, mommy?" he asked.

"Because, daddy and I love you very much and we're both so happy to have you in our lives." she replied almost in a whisper.

"Good," was his response as he continued eating the candied apple slices.

"Good," she repeated mentally.

She turned and began preparing scrambled eggs and toast for them both.

The more Sonya researched reincarnation, the more she wanted to talk to someone about it. She called her mother, without giving her details, only to find herself with more questions. Her mother did answer a few and to also lead her to an old friend who'd done some past life regression with a hypnotist. The "friend," had claimed to have been an Indian princess or priestess in a past life and went around boring everyone who spent more than a few minutes in her company. But, Sonya refused the phone number and thanked her mother anyway. She began instead to look up a hypnotist and simply ask a few simple questions.

The woman's voice was low and deep, almost like that of a male and for a moment Sonya almost laughed aloud but caught herself just in time.

"I have worked with youngsters in the past, my dear," she answered and slowly continued, "but children are not my specialty, "they tend to play games, you see."

"How old was the youngest," Sonya asked.

"Thirteen."

"How did that work out?"

"His was an old spirit, he had already lived numerous lives, you see."

"Numerous lives?"

"Yes dear, some of us live multiple lives until we get it right."

"I see."

"I hope that you do, dear. How old is this boy of yours?"

"Three, going on four next month," Sonya answered hesitantly.

"My dear, that's *too* young a mind to be regressing, I'm afraid I can't."

"Please Ms. Prim, please?"

"No dear, that's final!"

"Ms. Prim, I'll double the fee."

"My dear, what do you take me for? I don't do this for the money, that's secondary, *really*!"

"I'm sorry, I didn't mean to imply anything of the sort or insult! I'm, I'm just desperate to know more. You see, Mason is so sure of himself, and I must know!"

The line was quiet for a few seconds before Ms. Prim's response.

"I do know of a gentleman who might want to try his hand at this extraordinary request however, if he agrees, I would very much like to be in the room during the session or sessions if need be."

"Why yes, of course! Of, course! Thank you, Ms. Prim, thank you, so much!"

"I'll get back with you soon dear, goodbye."

Sonya decided not to tell Logan about the hypnotist after all, she didn't want to worry him or piss him off. She waited impatiently for the call but busied herself with more research. The more she read the more her curiosity grew to obsession.

"What if, Mason can't come back? What if, he becomes confused?" "What if, he doesn't want to do it?" "What if, what if?"

She'd been in the shower the morning the call came, so she'd missed it. As soon as she saw the missed call, she became apprehensive. Her hands trembled as she stared at the cell phone. "Is this the right thing to do?" she wondered.

"Oh my God, Logan will be *so* pissed off when he finds out I planned this!"

Sonya dialed the number.

Chapter Two

Dr. John Sullivan was a small, soft spoken man and Ms. Margaret Prim was tall, thin and walked with a no nonsense authority. When Sonya shook hands with Ms. Prim and finally Dr. Sullivan she felt surprisingly calm.

"May we meet the boy? Ms. Prim asked soon after formalities.

"I have a few questions before bringing Mason in," replied Sonya.

Dr. Sullivan smiled and simply stared at her, while Ms. Prim forced a smile.

"Please," Dr. Sullivan responded.

"I want to be sure Mason will be safe. I *need* to be sure he won't be harmed by this, it's just that I was so anxious to satisfy my curiosity that, I did not primarily take his safety into account, not that I'm a careless mother..."

"Sonya..."

"I'm not a bad mother."

"No one is questioning that, I assure you, Mason will be fine. I'll make sure of it!"

"Sonya," Ms. Prim interjects. "Your son will be fine. Dr. Sullivan is also a pediatrician, so Mason will be and is, in good hands."

"Thank you, it's just that I feel so...stup...."

"Please, no worries." the Doctor replied with a caring smile. "I'll simply ask a few questions to begin with and we'll go from there, ok?"

"Ok, ok...one more thing Doctor, may I call you John?"

"I'd prefer that."

"Ok, I'll bring him in."

"Mason, this is Ms. Margaret Prim and this is Dr. John Sullivan, they wanted to meet you and ask you a few questions, ok?"

"Hi." Mason nonchalantly shakes hands with the visitors while holding a small toy dinosaur tightly in the other hand.

"I see you like dinosaurs Mason, I love them. I have a room full of them at home."

Mason simply stared at the doctor's shoes and notices dinosaurs on the doctor's socks and points to them with a smile. "Oh, you caught me... I *told* you I *love* dinosaurs."

"Mason, your mom tells me that you were once married to her in Mexico, is that right?"

Mason nods in reply while biting his dinosaur's tail.

"Can we talk about that?" Mom, would you hold Mason on your lap?"

Sonya lifts Mason and he gently lays his head against her bosom and stares at the doctor.

"You can ask me anything you like while we talk. Ok?"

"Uh huh."

"I'd like you to listen to your mom's heartbeat. Just listen to her heartbeat as we talk, can you do that?"

Jason simply nods.

"What did you have for breakfast this morning?"

"Cereal and an apple."

"Good, if you feel like closing your eyes you can do that too."

Jason closes his eyes while he continues chewing on the toy.

All three patiently wait, as Mason listens and relaxes on his mother's lap. After a few minutes that seemed to last forever to Sonya, Mason begins to breathe contentedly.

"Mason, when you and your mommy lived in Mexico, you were married, is that true?"

Mason nods slightly.

"Tell me what Mexico looks like."

"It smells funny."

"What does it smell like?"

"Funny, not like it does at home."

"Do you remember the scent in your home, there in Mexico?"

"Smoke, and something else."

"Food?"

“I think so. Tortillas and, and poopy!”

Again, they all smile.

“I hope it’s not too bad.”

“Foochy.”

“What’s that?”

“Foochy.”

“Does that mean, it smells bad?”

“Uh huh.”

“That’s good, Mason. We can come back to that later, ok?”

“Ok.”

“What does your house look like?”

“Old.”

“Good, good.”

All three, smile as the doctor presses on.

“Mason, do you have family there?”

“I think so. I hear people talking and laughing.”

“Can you hear what they are saying?”

“No, it’s in another room, or outside.”

“Do you recognize any voices?”

“No, it’s too far.”

"Will you look outside and tell me what you see?"

"I can't get out of bed. My legs won't move."

"Is it sunny or cloudy?"

"Sunny."

"Hot?"

"Uh huh."

"Are you hungry?"

"Yes."

"Will you be eating soon?"

"Yes."

"I'd like to join you if I could?"

"Ok, there's a lot of food.

"Thanks Mason. Who's cooking?"

"Antonia."

"Your mommy?"

"No, she's not mommy."

"Who is she?"

"My...my...wife, my wife Tonia."

Sonya and Margaret stare at each other momentarily then turn their attention to John whose eyes were also closed.

"Mason..."

"Who is that?"

"Who am *I* talking to?"

"Me."

"Who are you?"

"I don't remember...my name."

"Alright, that's alright, tell me your name later, when you remember."

"Uh huh."

"What is Antonia doing now?"

"I'm thirsty."

"What is she doing?"

"Preparing a drink."

"That's very nice of her."

"She must."

"She must what?"

"Give me drink."

"May *I* have some drink?"

"Get your own."

"Ok, who do I ask?"

"Ask?"

"For a drink."

"Your woman!"

"And who is that?"

"What? Your woman estupido!"

"Es, what?"

"¡Estupido! ¡*Jajajaja*! Si *estupido!"*

All three are stunned. John looks at Sonya and waves his hand to calm her. Margaret stares unmoving. Sonya begins to shake and finally lifts Mason off her lap stares at his limp little body with tears in her eyes. John stands up and presses his hand to her shoulder while holding his finger to his mouth to silence and calm her. Sonya slowly shakes her head but does not move. John slowly presses down on her shoulder and she slowly lowers herself to the chair, placing Mason back on her lap and against her chest. She cries quietly not to awaken her sleeping boy.

"Have you eaten?"

"I am full."

"Tortillas?"

"¡Si, y mucho mas!"

"Will you answer me, in English please, I'm not very good at Spanish?"

"Of course, Inglich, whatever. I speak both."

Sonya's body shakes once more, but John's hand weighs heavy on her shoulder.

"Señor, Tonia is a beautiful woman."

"Si, cuidado, eh? ¡Tonia, es, brava!"

"She's brave, and crazy?"

"Yes."

"Oh, I see."

"Si, *jaja*!"

"Sir?"

"What? What?"

"Where in Mexico are we?"

"In the desert, my friend."

"Yes, but what desert?"

"Sonora, Mejico!"

"I want you to come home now."

"Thees ees, home."

"No, home to your home here in Texas, to your mother's home."

"No."

"No?"

"No. I am home, here."

"Come back home, come home, listen to your mommy's heartbeat, listen to her heartbeat."

John pauses long enough for Mason to respond to Sonya's beating heart.

"Mason, I want you to open your eyes when I touch your hand. I want you to remember where we are and remember where we've been. I want you to open your eyes when I touch your hand at the count of three. One...two...three.

"Mommy, I'm hungry."

John smiles at Sonya who smiles at Margaret who is sitting straight as a board with a tiny satisfied smile on her thin wrinkled lips.

Chapter Three

Logan could tell something was different with Sonya. He couldn't quite tell what, but something was a little different. She seemed happier and more vivacious, sexy. He looked at her with a yearning he hadn't felt in far too long a time. He wondered now why he hadn't felt more of this...this desire.

Sonya was brushing her hair, her mind on the unbelievable.

"Baby, Logan began, why don't we go out to dinner, just the two of us? Your mom could watch Mason, couldn't she?

Sonya's mind was elsewhere. She could hear Logan talking behind her but she ignored his words; he seemed to repeat himself a lot lately. She kept slowly brushing her hair, amazed on how smoothly John had done his work. She felt as though something dormant had awoken in her. Her heartbeat seemed to be stronger, faster, she could feel the beating behind her ears, hot, fluid, pouring down pulsating throughout her body, thunderously beating between her thighs. She found herself burning, burning...

"Baby? *Sonya, Sonya!"*

"What?" she answered annoyed.

"Didn't you hear me? What's gotten into you? I asked, if you'd like to go to dinner, just the two of us."

"Sure, just us..."

"Sonya, you're distracted. What's going on? Is everything ok?"

"Yeah, why not? I'm sorry, I was just thinking about Mason."

Is he ok? He's not sick or something, is he?"

No, he's fine, he's fine."

"Good, I can't stand it when he gets sick. Well, how about it? Dinner, you, me?

"Tomorrow night?"

"Call your mother, see if she can babysit."

"Ok, baby."

Sonya's mother, Elena was from the old country, she was born and raised in Laredo, Mexico and spoke English only when she had to. Elena had married a farm worker, a laborer who'd come and go, in and out of Mexico and the U. S. following the seasons. He'd been a good provider but he had women scattered throughout both countries and found it extremely difficult to break the habit even after marrying Elena. At first, she blamed herself as she wasn't familiar with the carnal pleasures her husband knew very well and thought herself inadequate. It took a few years and another man (during a long period of solitude when Javier had disappeared and was presumed dead as per rumors scattered about both countries not unlike the women in his life.) A man who convinced her that she was more than adequate. For some inexplicable and mysterious reason, something never understood by many in the world, Elena stayed with him through all those many years. Then the day of liberation finally came for both, when Javier was shot and killed in the bed of a long-time lover who they say was so old, no one in the town could believe she'd still been going at it. But, that had been some time back and in those years, Elena had found her cadre of gentlemen and not so gentlemen, to bring her up to speed in the carnal ways. Elena, being an older and wiser woman loved her freedom and did not much like babysitting, not even her own flesh and blood. Sonya had been an independent child which is why she had ended up marrying a white man. Another reason Elena did not like to babysit. She hated the idea of mixed babies. She knew it was wrong by some people's standards and ideas, but she could not reconcile the fact in her heart. She had disliked Logan from the moment her daughter had brought him home and she still disliked the man. Elena could not help her feelings and try as she might, just like her husband who couldn't keep his hands or his dick to himself, she could not break the habit.

When the babysitting request came, she came up with every excuse in the book and many others, to avoid the chore and a chore, it was!

"Mother, please watch Mason tonight only. You haven't seen or taken care of him, ever! Please do it! Please, mommy!"

Elena could not stand the idea of that poor half-breed being named Mason. Mason, what the hell kind of name is that for a half Mexican, half gringo? He was not a jar! And why did he have to be so pale? Son of a bitch, he was so pale!

"Ok, ok! *But don't make it a habit! Do you hear me, Sonya! I'm not a fucking babysitter and you are not going to turn me into one like all those "Viejas," in the neighborhood, whose daughters are "putas," having more babies for us to babysit! Tonight, and tonight only*! *Do you understand me*?"

"Thank you, mom. We'll be back before ten."

"You'd better, or you'll find him on your doorstep at ten-fifteen."

"See you tonight!"

"And tell that white man you married to not be late! *Fucking Gringo!"*

Sonya could not believe her luck she'd asked and begged her mother so many times in the past three almost four years until she'd finally stopped. She couldn't understand how her mother could reject her own flesh and blood. But, maybe this was the start of cracking that damn glacier. And what was up with that Gringo shit? At least Logan wasn't fucking all the women in and out of town like her own Dad had done.

"Oh no, what if he hadn't been her real dad? Oh, no, don't start that shit up Sonya!"

Logan was quite happy that the night was being a success. Sonya had laughed throughout the evening and seemed to be enjoying his company once again and, he was enjoying himself too. He still found it hard to believe she'd married him, a *Gringo*. She was so beautiful, a knockout and she'd said, *"Yes."*

He loved her with all his heart and could not see himself with any other woman, ever! He especially loved her smile, so radiant, so gorgeous. Yeah, he felt the luck of the Irish. The one person he'd hope would also love him was Elena. But, it was not meant to be. He'd come to the realization that you must take the bad with the good.

Elena stared at Mason as he watched Spanish language programming so intently, as though he understood what was being said. He'd laugh at the right moments and turn to look for her reaction when something inappropriate was being shown. It puzzled her because she knew that Sonya and that Gringo would not and could not teach him a language Logan did not know and Sonya garbled her way through. Still, she watched Mason and something deep and tiny inside of her solid cold uncaring heart began to warm. She found herself in the kitchen making refried beans and scrambled eggs while warming tortillas on the comal. Smiling to herself while, imagining Mason eating and talking in Spanish and speaking it well! Once as she swung around the dinner table she found a dance step she'd long ago left on a lonely dance floor in Mexico. The one she'd left behind when Javier (that no good bastard!) pulled her off, only to haul her into a little Godforsaken church in the deserts of Laredo with one old and blind witness and his two goats. But she found that dance step and many more as she made her way around the kitchen table. Soon she was sitting on the floor (rather uncomfortably) but next to a hungry child who seemed to appreciate her homemade tortillas and beans. He would look at her with those big innocent eyes and smile at her silliness and for a few moments she remembered how much fun Sonya had been those first precious years before she grew up and married that stupid white man.

Mason ate ravenously. Elena smiled and ran her hand through his thick curly hair. Mason jerked away momentarily and stared at his grandmother.

"Why do you hate me?" he asked her.

"Mijo, I don't hate you!"

"You don't come visit me and you call daddy names."

"I don't hate you. I don't like your daddy too much, but I don't hate you."

"Mommy and daddy say you hate me."

"What? Why would they tell you that?"

"They didn't tell me. I heard them."

"Mijo, you're a smart boy. I don't want you to say that or believe it. Ok? I love you."

"Why don't you like daddy?"

Elena found herself stumped. She stared at Mason for a while until he turned away to watch TV.

She stared at the back of Mason's head and wondered if she'd gone too far in not holding back on her anger. She felt stupid and angry at herself, just like she had when she was younger and ignored by Javier. Elena, walked into her bedroom, knelt at her bed just like she had as a child and prayed for forgiveness. When she stood, she saw Mason standing at the threshold of her door.

"Have you been watching me?"

"Yes."

"What are you thinking?"

"I want to go home."

Elena walked to him and embraced him in her thin arms. She picked him up and kissed his face and neck. Mason giggled and tried pulling away but Elena held him firmly, tightening her grip.

Elena moved to the bed and fell into it with Mason in her arms. They lay there for a long time not saying a word.

"Grandma? Will you babysit me again?"

"Yes, my love. I will. I promise, I will."

Once home, Logan rushed to the bathroom and began to clean up, excited with the thought of having a couple of baby free hours in bed with the love of his life. He felt like a fidgety teenager once more causing him to laugh aloud.

Sonya in the meantime had volunteered to open that bottle of wine they'd stored since Mason's birth. She was pulling the cork when she suddenly stopped and the thought of Mason and John and the session came back to mind. Holding the bottle opener in her hand she stared as in a trance at nothing. She stood frozen in place as the memories of that day flooded her thoughts. Time was no more as

Mason's voice laughing and speaking with a funny Mexican accent brought a torrent of tears and an uncontrollable shaking of her body until she could no longer stand and fell to the kitchen floor.

Logan half dressed, found Sonya unconscious.

He carried her to bed and called Elena, who did not answer.

Elena rushed into the emergency room carrying Mason on her hip. She was angry and in shock. Her eyes locked into Logan's eyes and gave him a look of hatred unlike any she'd given before. Logan winced but gathered the courage to go to her and take Mason into his arms (hoping she wouldn't take a swing at him while holding his son). Elena without a word snatched Mason back and placed him on her hip as before. She stormed over to the receptionist's desk and asked for Sonya. Logan watched her disappear into the ward.

"Sonya, wake up. Sonya, do you hear me? Wake up m'ija."

Sonya responded with a murmur that Elena could not hear or understand.

"Sonya, it's time to wake up and take care of your baby."

Logan came into the crowded area where several patients lay waiting for, who knows what? He was nervous and scared to see his beautiful wife like this. He realized that Mason should not be here and began to take him from Elena's arm. She turned and without warning slapped his face causing him to cry out and wince in pain. Elena quickly turned back around. Logan angrily pulled on Mason's arm making him cry and scream in pain. Elena spun around and tried slapping Logan once more. He was prepared this time lifting his arm in defense. Elena swung hard two more times until a pair of orderlies pulled her away and took them both out of the ward and out onto the driveway keeping a watch on them until guards arrived.

"She's my wife and I need to be with her," Logan cried out to one guard. This is her mother, she's angry and attacked me when I tried to take my son out of there!"

"Look sir," the guard replied either she or you can see your wife, but you're right, your son should not be in there. "Now you two have got to resolve this or neither one of you can go in, got that?"

Elena slowly walked over to Logan and did something she'd never done before. She apologized.

Logan, fearing a trick of some kind, did not move and stood in place for a few frightful moments before handing Mason over to her and nodding his head in understanding. He walked off to see about Sonya.

After a couple of hours, Sonya managed to awaken and ask for Mason. Logan explained what had taken place and left her to send Elena in.

It took about thirty minutes before Elena came to tell Logan the doctor was releasing Sonya and they could go home. He was shocked once again when she offered to take Mason with her for the night. Logan than did something he'd never contemplated in his life he walked over and hugged Elena, kissing her on the cheek.

Chapter Four

Logan was pissed. He was so angry with Sonya he could not look at her.

"Why didn't you tell me? Why did you do that?" Why would you not tell me?"

"I don't know."

"What do you mean?

"I thought you wouldn't agree and you'd stop me."

"Of course, I'd stop you! Why wouldn't I?"

"You don't understand..."

"Fuck that!"

"Please don't be angry, Logan. I had to do it."

"No! You didn't have to do shit! You wanted to and you did!"

"Logan, he spoke Spanish."

"Bullshit! That's bullshit and you know it!"

"He spoke Spanish. He called his wife Antonia, Tonia."

"That's a crock of shit, Sonya!"

"He did. He remembered. He saw Mexico, he *was* in Mexico!"

Sonya sat next to John while Margaret held Jason in her long thin arms. Mason felt out of place but he smiled at Margaret as she bounced him on her bony knees.

END

RE-BECCA

Becca, my love, was suffering, I had no idea what to do! She lay on the bed propped up, several pillows supported her upper body, she groaned continually, causing me to feel more helpless. I had no choice but to make the call.

Two ladies entered our bedroom and immediately set to work on my Becca. They were both gentle and rough on her. One lifted her head and removed the pillows in one swift motion the other, removed her undies and spread her legs apart. It shocked and angered me to see her treated that way. I had never treated her like that! My heart and soul were vested in her care. Becca completely trusted me with her life. Our love had grown immensely since our union. There was nothing I would deprive her of and my love for her was fierce. Becca knew my love was genuine and I understood her love for me as well. Caregivers had no idea and few understood what we have gone through to survive.

One of the caregivers asked me to leave the room, as they had to open her up for a more thorough diagnosis. This turned helplessness to fear. It is one thing to feel incapable of support but to now feel such fright was unbearable. What would they do to her? What if there was nothing they could do for her? What if this was the end of my Becca? I ran to my bar and poured me a double scotch and worried on my recliner. The wait was unbearable. I walked to the bedroom door, and pressed my ear to it hoping to hear something, anything that would ease my fear and impatience. I drank two more doubles and felt them hit me hard. My mind was a blur of worry and remorse. I should have taken her for a checkup sooner, as any good partner would have done. Why had I ignored her first complaints? Why didn't I stop my work long enough to have listened to her? Nothing would change that now. Now, it might be too damn late!

I don't remember how long it took for one of the caregivers to wake me but, it was now dark. I splashed my face with cold water at the bar's sink and towel dried my face before focusing on her eyes.

"Mr. Marquez, we've done all that we can here. I've requested an ambulance. It should be here any moment."

"What have you learned? What is wrong with her? *Would you please, tell me?"* I cried out! She means so much to me. I don't know what I'd do without her anymore. *"What's wrong with her?"*

"Mr. Marquez, I'd rather you reserve your questions for the..."

"NO! Absolutely not! Tell me now!" Tell me!

"She has an abnormality. *I have no idea how to explain it. This is the most unusual thing my assistant and I have ever seen!* Nothing like this has ever happened before."

"Abnormality. What do you mean, an abnormality? What kind of abnormality?"

"Sir, she's...pregnant. Somehow she grew a womb. She's six weeks pregnant."

"Pregnant? A womb, but how is that possible? I thought..."

"We don't know, that's why she has to get to the lab right away. The techies will have to do a more thorough examination."

"Thorough examination, you mean they'll have to *cut her up*, don't you? *No! No! No! I won't let you do that! No one can touch her! No one!* Call them off. I don't want them here. Do you understand? *Call them off!*"

"Mr. Marquez, I assure you, she'll be in good hands and in the best of care. You've been cleared to attend the procedure. I knew you'd be surprised if not shocked by the discovery, so I requested your presence throughout the procedure."

My heart was beating wildly, my mind raced with the possibilities! I'd be a father -- if things went well, I'd be a, *Father!*

The ambulance raced to the laboratory as I held Becca's hand. I'd whispered the news into her ear as her eyes rolled behind closed lids. I was excited yet much calmer. The idea of becoming a father soothed anxiety, and now at least I knew what Becca's condition was. My hand gripped hers tightly as we raced to the lab.

The surgical room was only large enough for maybe six people. I was not allowed. My viewing area was on a bleacher-like bench above them. I could see everything from this bird's-eye view. The lead caregiver sat next to me after handing me a cup of coffee. She sipped on her own with a look of anticipation in her eyes.

"Mr. Marquez?"

"Xavier, please."

"Xavier, nothing like this has ever happened. In our field, nothing of this magnitude. This is quite literally, a *miracle*..."

"A miracle, Miss? Aren't miracles reserved for humanity?"

"BECCA, is human too. I thought that you were aware of that, since you've owned her for so long."

"Yes, I suppose you're right. She is more human than any purely biological woman I've ever known. I don't see her as a possession but as a partner, a wife, *my wife*."

"What is amazing is that these, "Biologically Enhanced Computer Controlled Automatons," were never produced with human reproductive organs. Somehow, your BECCA, has grown not only multiple fully functioning organs, but they do what human organs naturally do. Her womb has a mutation of some kind growing in it. *This is historical in every sense of the word!"*

"Baby... she has a baby in her womb, not a mutation."

"Mr. Marquez, we don't know for sure what she has created, *what you both have created!"*

"It's called a *child*, a life, a baby."

"Yes, of course, a baby."

My Becca was going to be a mother. The thought was so invigorating! My mind raced with the possibilities of a family.

"Xavier, Mr. Marquez?"

My child, my baby, what would we call him or her? Who would the baby look like I wondered?

"Mr. Marquez, Mr. Wong would like to see you, he needs to speak with you."

"Hello, Mr. Wong." Can you please tell me how Becca is? Will she be able to birth our baby? Will you help us?"

"Mr. Marquez, I wish I could answer all of your questions, at this moment I have no idea. This is new for us, no one has ever heard, much less seen anything quite like this." Frankly, I have to consult with the board of directors..."

"Board of directors, what are you saying?"

"Mr. Marquez, for us to continue further, we must notify the board, speak with our attorneys!"

"Wait, wait, she's mine! I paid for her she's mine, you no longer have the authority to do anything without my consent!"

"Mr. Marquez, you still owe quite a bit on this model. You are mistaken. Technically she still belongs to the corporation. She is not fully paid for, she's on credit."

"No wonder you wanted to have her brought here, you knew this before you brought her here. *What will you do now, throw me out?"*

"Mr. Marquez, I ask that you understand the gravity of this unusual situation. Nothing like this was ever imagined, by anyone. This is a most important development, *unprecedented in this or any other field of robotics, or science for that matter!"*

"Will the company allow us to remain a family? I love Becca and I know she wants us to remain a family, Mr. Wong, will you assure me that we will remain a family?"

"I will do my best to convince the board that it would be best for the corporation to allow you this."

"Thank you, Mr. Wong. I'll take you at your word and place my BECCA in your hands."

At home, I waited for several days to hear from Mr. Wong. I began regretting my decision, wondering whether I should have trusted him. I had run out of Scotch and dressed to run to the liquor store downstairs when my doorbell rang. I opened the door and there standing before me was Becca. She smiled the most heavenly smile and placed her arms around me.

I awoke early in the morning and carefully examined her body. She had the same scars and marks I'd come to know. There was one difference, one scar was redone perfectly; however, it was done in reverse.

One on her left hand, the one which I'd accidently cut with a paring knife when I reached into the dishwasher at the same time she had, and sliced her hand in the process.

I knew this BECCA was a replacement. I was also aware, that the corporation had sent her to appease me. They would never allow me to have her back. They now held my Becca against my will and along with her, our baby.

END

FILLING STATION

Lydia drove past the old abandoned filling station several times when she first moved into the neighborhood, it always made her smile recalling her childhood days. Her father had been a shade tree mechanic since his teen years and was eventually hired on as a fulltime mechanic at a filling station, like this one. It was tiny and yet, in those days seemed huge in her youthful glimmering eyes. She recalled the people who'd stop to fill up or drop off their cars and motorbikes. The neighborhood kids would stop and visit for a while before asking her dad for pieces of black tire rubber for use in patching their bicycle's flat tires. Her curiosity made her investigate the service station's history and later, she bought it.

I was driving through the neighborhood when I first saw Lydia painting the front door of that gas station. I drove by at least five times before I built up my courage to stop and talk. I introduced myself and although very busy, she took the time to talk with me. I told her that I admired the old building and had always had dreams of buying and renovating one just as she was now doing. She put the paint brush down and stopped to look me squarely in the eyes. I could tell she was curious, yet hesitant.

"Ben, what is it about old filling stations that you like?" she asked.

"The memories," I replied. "My father worked in one when I was a little boy and I remember how he used to make everyone smile even when he was forced to tell someone that their car was just too worn out to fix anymore."

Lydia smiled and nodded her head. She turned, picked up the brush and continued painting.

I also told her how when my father would get home, my mother would sit him down and clean his hands, fingernails and his face. She would bring a bowl of hot water, a piece of cloth or an old ragged towel, a bar of hard soap and rub him clean.

My father would stare at her and marvel at her love of him. She would take a nail file and clean his nails of the grease and grime. I'd untie his boots and pull them off looking up at him to see his approval and wink. Those boots stank like hell, I'd take them and place them just outside the front door and later just before bedtime, I'd collect them and put them under the chair next to their bed. My father would put a coin or two on the chair for me and I'd always end up spending those coins at his filling station.

Lydia smiled broadly the whole time I spoke. Her smile was small and knowing. It was as if she understood my history and accepted it without question. Instinctively I reached for a brush and began painting right alongside of her. She didn't stop me.

When the door was done, Lydia looked it over and clapped her hands together shouting, "Yes!" I smiled, nodding in agreement.

As she locked up, I asked if she'd like a beer. I regretted asking when she looked at me and hesitated. I apologized a bit embarrassed and began to walk away.

"Hey! Where you headed?" she asked.

"Down the street, to Belle's Icebox, she's got ice cold beer."

"Yes, I've seen it, I'll see you there."

Belle smiled and put down a cold "Lonestar" in front of me.

"What are you grinning about Benny?" "You look like a kid who's gotten away with something."

"I think I found my wife, Belle." I replied with a silly smile.

"Now that's funny!" Belle laughed as she waddled away.

Lydia showed up after about an hour. She had changed into a clean t-shirt and a pair of short shorts, which showed off her long, tanned legs. Her smile was bigger than it had been earlier and it made me grin just as much. Belle came by took her order and winked at me as she swayed her large hips like a model, in a teasing way. Lydia had seen the wink and laughed quietly as she looked at me. I must have blushed because she laughed out loud. I felt stupid guilty and looked away. Lydia punched my arm and pulled my sleeve towards her. I looked deeply into her eyes and swore, I could read her thoughts.

"What did you tell her?" she asked coyly.

"Just that, I'd met my future wife." I whispered.

"Wife? So, you plan on marrying me?

"I, I . . .," I stuttered.

"You're bold."

"Sorry," I managed to whisper.

"Loosen up, Ben. It's ok." I think that was cute"

"I'm an idiot."

"Well, give it time I'll see if I agree." she teased laughing once again.

As we talked and drank more beer, we spoke a bit about our childhoods. When she told me that her father had managed a filling station too, I nearly fell off my stool!

Lydia's mother died shortly after birthing her, she was raised by her father. He'd been a great father she said, "The best!" Tears welled up in her eyes and her cheeks flushed as she reminisced. He'd gotten sick just before she graduated from high school and never recovered. He died just as she began her young adult life. He'd been wise enough to save and had left her a nice sum of money which she used to move away from her hometown and eventually end up in Houston. She worked at an oil firm and was doing well for herself. She knew her father would be very proud. I listened and wanted to learn more. She eventually stopped and asked me to tell her about myself.

"I miss Mexico, I told her. We were poor and my father learned to repair cars and all kind of machinery from his father and uncles. It was our grandfather who bought a small filling station after many years and my father worked there until he couldn't. I was the youngest of seven children my father was already old when I was born. He was sixty-three when my mother had me. She was a Yaqui Indian who managed to escape from her family; she said they had always treated her like a slave. She left her parent's house and became a slave to her own family."

"What do you mean?" Lydia asked.

"Well, taking care of seven kids and having a husband who demanded everything of her, took its toll on her."

"Is she alive?

"No, she died years ago, I replied lowering my head. She and I left Mexico long ago. My father was extremely angry with us for crossing the border. None of my brothers wanted to work the filling station and his hopes died when I left for good. He sent word with a cousin that he had disowned us, as if my mother and I had been his possessions all along."

We both grew silent.

"You're quite the Texan," she said with a smile. "Lonestar beer in an icehouse with a bunch of rednecks.

I laughed and gently poked her side. "Well, I've been Mexican all my life and Texan a few years." "My English is not that good. But I do try.

"I don't think the Mexican will ever completely leave you," she said.

"I hope not."

"Especially that accent," she laughed while poking my ribs.

"I don't want it to go away."

"Tell me more about your Yaqui Indian mom."

"No, let's talk about your mom."

"I didn't know her. All I know is what my father told me about her." Lydia looked sad once again.

"Ok, let's talk about your filling station. Why did you buy it?"

"It reminds me of my father."

"That's all?"

"Yes, that's all."

"You bought it because of nostalgia?"

"Probably."

"Another cerveza?"

"No more cervezas, I'm done! Time to go."

Lydia grabbed my shoulder, pushed herself away from me and walked off. I watched as she skipped a step, like a happy little girl. I felt the urge to run after and stop her. I didn't and watched her drive away.

A week passed before I pulled up to the filling station and saw everything she'd painted in that short time. She heard my truck and looked over her shoulder waving hello, with the brush.

"Took you a while to come back," she said coyly.

"I had to leave town, deliver parts to a friend in Corpus."

"I thought you'd decided there was too much work to do around here and changed your mind about helping."

"Oh, I thought about it. Then I said to myself. Hey! Who could walk away from a boss as good as that?"

"Good as that? What exactly is *that*?"

"As good as a cold beer in a dry sand storm in West Texas."

"That good, huh?"

"Better," I smiled.

"Wow, now that's impressive. Did you think of that all by yourself?"

"No, I got it off a billboard in Amarillo." I just thought, it would make you laugh, and angry at the same time."

"Yes and no. Yes, because you think I'm "as good as *that*," and no because you're an asshole for wanting me like a bottle of beer."

"*A cold beer*, dry dust storm, West Texas."

"You're still an asshole."

"So, would you like me to hold you like a cold beer?"

"Let me think about it."

"Don't think too long, I may decide to leave for another week."

"You're such a male tease."

I walked over and wrapped my arms around her waist. She was hot and sweaty, but that was fine. I kissed her cheek then her lips, she kissed me gently then as hard as she could. I felt her teeth mash against mine.

I pressed the putty knife deep into decades-old grease on the driveway, a place where countless automobiles had been reborn and others died, and hauled off for scrap. The black grease spots on the old cracked concrete reminded me of the age spots on my mother's hands. The long dry rust stains reminded me of the dried blood left on the floor boards of the old shack where I'd cleaned up, after finding my mother's body. A drunk old white doctor had coldly told her that she had cancer and there was nothing to be done, it was too late. He scolded her for not seeing a doctor sooner. She went home, wrote me a letter and stabbed herself in the heart. When I got home, and found her, I screamed and fell to my knees to lift her, her tiny body was already cold when I held her in my arms. I first thought, someone had attacked her. I found her letter just before the police arrived. I had never felt such pain. No matter how much I try to put it out of my mind, I can't. I keep blaming myself for her death. If I'd only stayed and not come to this country, she would have seen a doctor in Mexico and she'd be alive.

Tears fell on my hand as I pushed the putty knife deeper into the grease. My hands now reminded me of my father's scarred and strong ones. I pictured my mother wiping them as clean as she could. I remember him reaching up to caress her cheek and hold her eyes in his. The memory only released more tears. I quietly sniffled hoping Lydia would not hear.

"Ben, are you ok?"

I nodded, and wiped my nose against my sleeve, then wiped my eyes with the other. I couldn't look at her. I knew if I did, I'd start to cry like a child, so I nodded and kept scraping. Thankfully, she walked away quietly.

"Were you thinking about your mom?" Lydia asked a little later.

"Yes, *and* my father," I replied

"I thought of my father too, when I saw you scraping the driveway with that little putty knife. For a moment, I saw him."

"You did?"

"Well, not *him*, you reminded me of him in that instant. I did a double take and realized I'd seen a memory."

"I'm glad."

"Me too," she said, tenderly kissing the top of my head.

Later that night we held each other tightly, standing on that old stained driveway. Remembering our past, and praying for a better future.

END

FROZEN FOR LATER

This is not what I paid for!

I sought to wake up in the future, many decades into the future where it would be possible to overcome any disease, even death. I chose cryogenics for this reason alone. *Yes, I chose to be frozen!*

I said my goodbyes to loved ones, left them a huge part of my fortune so that they may live comfortably without worry or concern for themselves or me. They must have had happy and fruitful lives. That was a huge part of my plan.

Now I wonder if I may be looking at my own *future* relatives.

We cannot communicate, I've done my best to speak slowly and gesture in simple and grotesque ways and yet, nothing seems to work. Why don't they give me something to write with? Don't they write? The lack of ears, nose, lips and small jaws must be the cause. In fact, while they curiously eye me, I watch and study them. I've never heard them speak or make a sound of any type. They must be beyond words for communication. I never see them come and go, they just simply appear and disappear as if, by will. Is this, what we humans have evolved to? Should I even consider them as human? Are they? Maybe they're a genetic mutation? Or, maybe they're not human at all? They simply stand before me and stare transfixed, as though I'm the freak!

Well, they've never touched or probed me as I know we'd do if the shoe was on the other foot, so to speak. Well no, I'm wrong they had to have touched me to get me out of the cryogenic container. They somehow managed to revive me and place me in this . . . this . . .cell?

Occasionally I see the smaller ones arrive with taller beings. They seem to be afraid of me. They gesture slowly and move their heads in odd ways and cover their mouth hole, which I believe might be shock or fear. It's odd but when the small ones are present, I believe that I can actually feel their emotions. The taller ones never react. I believe they don't wish me to know their thoughts or feelings. What could they be afraid of?

This area in which I am kept has no bars and I have no restraints to hold me back yet, every time I move towards my observers, a heavy and pliant like force holds me back.

Although it's there, it's invisible. A barrier that, not even a scent penetrates. I say that because I can't smell a thing! Nothing! It's one of the oddest sensations I've ever experienced. The air is scentless, I am scentless, or at least what I once smelled like, I no longer do. All of my senses work perfectly fine. My nose *can* smell, I know because on occasion, I catch a faint whiff of a peculiar scent, impossible to recognize, nothing I recall. Where it emanates from is also impossible to tell. Is it a memory? Is my mind toying with me?

My only nourishment has been a sort of thick milky white paste devoid of flavor. They must have no idea of spices or condiments. I haven't had a drop of water for ages it seems. It does keep me full and refreshed in an odd way. No matter how much or how little of it I eat, I am neither hungry nor thirsty afterwards. I first refused to have any of it, as I wasn't sure what it was made of or what it was for. Besides, I never was one for milk or dairy products. A nice Chianti or frothy dark beer, now that's the ticket! It sat there for a long period and it didn't smell of anything familiar and it never seemed to change color or smell rancid, so I finally grew ravenous and ate a tiny portion and as I mentioned earlier, I felt nourished. I've been eating it consistently even though I now suspect that it may contain some sort of medication. I wonder if these...these...people? Do they eat the same paste they provide me? Are they, people? Should I consider them people? Their tiny apertures may not have lips but they could easily use a straw of sorts.

Are there others like me anywhere near? Maybe, they're holding someone right next to my cell and I just can't hear them? I screamed loudly several times at first, to no effect. They simply stood and watched with concern and interest. They chose to ignore me and simply watched my anger sometimes one or two would pantomime my behavior.

If there are others like me, will they ever bring us together as an experiment of some type? No, probably not. I must be the only specimen of my kind here. I must be.

There is no sense of time in these confines. No windows to let in the sun or moonlight. I remember the sun. I miss sunlight! Why isn't there at least one damn window! Give me something to see, you bastards!

Try as I might, nothing scratches here! I want to write! Something! Anything! What the hell is everything made of? I can't mark my days, weeks, months or time anywhere!

Days? Time? What the hell is wrong with me? How can I mark time if I have no idea how it passes? What happened to my watch? What the fuck does it matter? Wait! Wait! My heartbeat! I can take time by monitoring my heartbeat! No, that's too tedious. I can feel it and I can hear it with this damn silence but I can't write on anything! What the hell is wrong with me? There is no time here, only a memory of time exists for me. They are going to release me, aren't they?

I see now, how constricting the concept of time was back then. Back then; that sounds so screwed up. Back then. Back then. Ha! That thought alone is laden with time.

Back then, back then, back when, back when, whenever, whenever, ever since, since then, since then, then, then, back then, back when I...

I haven't slept...I haven't slept for; how long? I hadn't thought of it until now! Why did I just remember that? I haven't slept. How could I forget to sleep? How could my body forget? I don't feel tired or sleepy. How could I forget sleep? I know! I know! I'm not on earth! I can't be! On earth we feel the push and pull of the sun and moon, of heavenly bodies! That must be why I don't tire! Why I don't sleep...isn't it? Or is it that milky crap they keep feeding me? Why do I keep eating that shit? I'm never hungry! Yet, every time they bring it here I stuff it in my mouth! Flavorless shit! I won't touch it anymore! I refuse to eat it! I won't eat it! *Do you hear me, you, freaks? I won't eat it anymore! I'll die first! I'll die! See how you like that, huh? I won't be your little caged monkey, anymore! You, fucking jailers!* Jailers. Damn jailers... I'm not your monkey specimen...Or am I? Am I your hairy ape in a cage? Your hairy ape? Hair...hair...my hair...hair...my hair...My hair! It's not there! It's gone. I'm bald! What happened to my hair? All my hair is gone. *Give me a mirror you, fucks! Give me a goddamn mirror!* Why would you take my hair? Why? I had a great head of hair...Thick, shiny. Commanding! I always received compliments on it... Why would you take it? *May I have a goddamn mirror? Please? A mirror please?* Don't you even know what that is? Nothing reflects here, nothing...

How long have I been here? *Hello? Hello? Anyone? Anyone out there?* There I go again. There is no time here, you, stupid ape! No concept of time here. Only memories of time...time when...time when...When what? What? When what? What was I saying? Who was I talking to? *Is anyone listening? Hello?* Hell no...I feel like I'm losing it. I can't seem to remember my past...my memory is slipping...slipping...spilling...spilling into oblivion...Hahaha! Slipping, spilling, spitting, splitting, pity, pity, pity, pity me...ha ha ha...What was I saying? Who's laughing at me? Who's there? Hello?

My mother, I remember my mother! She had long black hair. She smiled with huge beautiful pearly white teeth! She was the love of my life, my wife...she died of cancer, my wife died of cancer...my mother did too. They both died of candor, condor, they took flight like a condor with cancer...cantor...she sang like a bird of paradise...pair of dice...I threw the dice and I chose to be frozen for the future...future...I fly like a bird too...I fly to the future...my dream came to... no, my dream came true...true dream...dream...dreamcicle...icicle...icicle...ice cream...I scream, you scream we all scream for dream schemes! Hmmm, hmmm, hmmm...

My sons warned me! They warned me! They said, if you do it, if you do it... just do it! You'll...you'll...be forgotten cause, you'll be rotten...to the core...and you'll be no more...My sons said, you'll miss the sun...they said...you'll be dead anyway...what do they know? How could they know? My sons...What was that? Who? Who are you? Who are...who are...who are...you? *Yoo-hoo! Yoo-hoo! Coo Coo! Who's there? Are you there? Are you watching me go coo coo? Who, who?*

Where am I again? Why me? Why me? It's all about me...me...me...Isn't it? It's about me. I said so. I said so...I told you so...told you...so...so they told me. So, they told me...

Is this a dream? Yes...I choose to dream...

I bought myself a ticket. I bought it, I deserve to do it. I wanted to live forever...forever...I bought the ticket...to forever...Didn't I? But why? Why not?

Didn't I? Buy? Bye, bye...

Why? Why me? Me. Me what?

Who? Who said that? Who?

Wha? Wh?

?????

What is that? What the...? It's me...*it's me!*

How can I be there? How can I see myself? I know it's me, it's me. *Of course, it's me!* I'm holding hands with one of the creatures...or is it holding my hand? Why am I smiling at me? How can I be there and here?

Oh, God! They've cloned me! That's what it is! It's my clone!

Wait...my hands. *Where are my hands? Where are my arms? Where am I?*

Ahhhhhhahhhhhhahhhhhh! Ahhhhhhahhhhhhahhhhhh! Ahhhhhhahhhhhhahhhhhh!

They stole my body and left my mind here! Wherever here may be...

You asked for this, remember? You wanted to live forever, remember?

Now you will, now you will...

END

ABOUT THE AUTHOR

Manuel Nava Leal has been creating and writing stories and poetry, entertaining family and neighborhood friends since childhood, in South Texas. His passion is the short story, he has transformed several into theatrical productions. Mr. Leal has been involved in theater 40+ years.

On occasion, Mr. Leal is invited to participate in acting and writing workshops in schools around Houston and surrounding communities, relishing the opportunity of bringing the written word and theater to youth of all ages.

Manuel enjoys reading immensely, his creative influences come from a wide range of authors such as; P. Neruda, R. Anaya, R. Hinojosa, A. Hitchcock, A. Huxley, S. Maugham, E. A. Poe, R. Serling, T. Welty, K. Vonnegut N. Hawthorne, O. Henry, and many others.

Other books by the author:

One Tejano's Throe - Short Stories and Poetry (Self-published 2005)

Beautiful Heart - A collection of Romantic Poetry (Creative House Publishing 2007)

Mysterious Memories – Short Stories (Creative House Publishing 2009)

Shattered and Scattered – Poetry (Creative House Publishing 2011)

Blue Agave Imaginings is the recent collection of short stories from the talented author/playwright, Manuel Nava Leal. Author of "One Tejano's Throe" (2005) "Beautiful Heart a Collection of Romantic Poetry" (2007) "Mysterious Memories" (2009) and Shattered and Scattered 2011)

Blue Agave Imaginings carries one through the universe on explorations far from the average world we believe to understand. Tales that compel one to imagine worlds of possibilities and witness infinite impossibilities.

Manuel Nava Leal once again, carries his readers on imaginary travels to marvelous locales, from the depths of space to the foundations of one's soul. Imaginings that may not be quite what they appear to be at first glance. Find out for yourself, enjoy the journeys!